I0715516

"The well-crafted storyline makes this a worthwhile read. Stuffed with gratuitous sex and over-the-top violence, this novel has a riveting plot."
KIRKUS REVIEWS

"Verdict: The pacing is relentless in this debut, a hard-boiled novel with a shocking ending. The supershort chapters will please those who enjoy a James Patterson–style page-turner"
LIBRARY JOURNAL

A "clever and engrossing mystery tale involving gorgeous women, lustful men and scintillating suspense."
FOREWORD REVIEWS

"Part of what makes this thriller thrilling is that you sense there to be connections among all the various subplots; the anticipation of their coming together keeps the pages turning."
BOOKLIST

"Guaranteed to keep you reading, this is one of the best thrillers I've read yet."
NEW MYSTERY READER MAGAZINE

"A superb thriller and an exceptional read."
MIDWEST BOOK REVIEW

"Verdict: This fast-paced book offers fans of commercial thrillers a twisty, action-packed thrill ride."
LIBRARY JOURNAL

"Another masterpiece of action and suspense."

WORTH A SHOT

THRILLER PUBLISHING GROUP, INC.

WORTH
A SHOT

JIM MICHAEL HANSEN
R.J. JAGGER

THRILLER PUBLISHING GROUP, INC.

WORTH A SHOT

Thriller Publishing Group, Inc.
Golden, CO 80401

Copyright©JimMichaelHansen

ISBN 978-1-954518-37-7

Printed in the United States of America

For Eileen

ACKNOWLEDGEMENTS

Thanks to the many wonderful people who played a part in making this happen. Special appreciation goes out to Dani Bash who did brave battle to find and remove a truckload of stubborn little typos and errors.

Special appreciation also goes out the extraordinarily talented people who created the amazing audiobook version of this title (under the name Shot of Love), inclucing Roger Rittner, Daniel Chodos, Robin Riker, J.W. Terry, Christopher Cabrera, Bob Lynes, Al Johnson and Scene One Media.

DAY ONE

July 7
Wednesday

1

Nick Teffinger, the 34-year-old head of Denver's homicide unit, woke Wednesday morning to find himself in a cheap hotel room, with light from a strong sun squirting around a frayed vinyl blind. It was mid-morning, long past when he should already be at work. The sound of a running shower came from behind a closed bathroom door.

His brain was a wreck.

It was the victim of too many beers and shots and wee hours and drunken sex.

He muscled into a vertical position and swung his legs over the edge of the bed. The gray matter inside his cranium responded with a dull swirl. On the floor lay a bra and a white sundress. On the shade of a lamp across the room hung a pink thong. Seeing it, he had a vague recollection of waving it over his head like a victory flag and throwing it in that direction.

Last night was a blur.

He vaguely remembered the woman, with her surfer-blond hair and her surfer-girl body, and up top, that face, that love-me-do or love-me-don't face. He remembered trying to not fall for her when he first saw her sitting there at the bar. He remembered telling himself to just do what he went there to do and then get home to a sensible night's sleep, but then came the first beer—"just one"—followed by the causal toss of the woman's hair and her oh-so-easy smiles and the way she came in tight when he slipped a bill in the jukebox and pulled her off the stool for a slow dance.

What was her name again?

Janie?

Joanie?

Something like that—

A large black purse lay dead at the foot of a nightstand, either fallen there or dropped in a heat of passion, with a pink wallet spilling halfway out. One quick peek, that's all he'd take, just enough to get the woman's name.

He pulled out the wallet.

Inside was an Illinois driver's license for one Jackie Jones. Seeing the captivating face staring back at him, he remembered her name now, Jackie, and even more remembered the reason he had to have her in his life the moment he saw her.

Under the wallet was something that caught his breath, something that he most definitely didn't expect.

It was a gun.

He pulled it out and took a closer look. It was Sig 9mm with serious stopping power, fully loaded. Under it he found yet something else, namely a large envelope with three or four rubber bands around it. He took a peek inside to find money, lots of money, all in fifty and hundred dollar bills. He guessed it was somewhere between twenty and thirty grand.

Nothing else out of the ordinary was in there.

He put everything back exactly as he'd found it and stood up. His legs wobbled but were steady enough to not let him drop.

He went into the bathroom and pulled back the shower curtain.

Inside, lathering up, was the most beautiful woman he'd ever seen.

2

Teffinger had had women before, more than his fair due, but this one—*this one*, it was as if she'd sprung directly out of the secret corners of his brain where he stored images and songs and feelings and emotions and all the great little things that were worth getting into your life and holding them tight, if you only could.

She pulled him into the shower, rubbed her stomach against his and put her arms around his neck. Then she said, "Baby, don't look at me like that."

"Like what?"

"Like there's more."

The words landed hard.

He said, "I thought I'd call in sick today . . ."

She smiled but didn't soften.

"It was nice, last night. But I'm just passing through. I told you that. You knew it was a one night thing, going into it."

He remembered now.

She was only in Denver for the night, en route to someplace that wasn't Denver.

"Stick around for awhile," he said.

She shook her head.

"Maybe in out next lives. Right now, I need to get on the road."

"To where, again?"

"Los Angeles."

"Right, yeah."

She ran a finger down his nose.

"Sorry, baby. Last night was fun though, it really was. I'll never forget it."

His chest pounded.

"Look," he said. "You got to eat. At least let me get you some breakfast."

She considered it.

Then she said, "What the fuck— It has to be quick, though. Scrub my back, will you?"

3

Over pancakes and coffee at Eats for Eaters, a dive mom-without-pop restaurant fifty steps down Colfax, the food equivalent of the fleabag room, Teffinger said, "I don't know anything about you."

She leaned across the table and whispered.

"You know I make noise."

He smiled.

"That's true."

"And you know my name, unless you forgot it."

"Jackie," he said.

"Do you remember my last name?"

"Jones."

She smiled.

"Look at you with all those memory cells. I'm impressed."

He had to keep her in Denver; that was his one and only thought. If she left, he'd get over it, sure, but he'd always wonder what would have happened, if.

"So what's in Los Angeles?"

"I don't know yet."

"You don't?"

She shook her head.

"Have you ever been there before?"

"No."

"So why are you going, exactly?"

"To meet someone."

"A boyfriend?"

She laughed at the concept. "No."

"A friend?"

"No."

"Who then?"

"I don't know yet."

"You're going there to meet somebody and you don't know who it is?"

"That's right."

"A specific person or someone in general?"

"A specific person."

"And then what happens after you meet this person?"

"That's for me to know."

Teffinger took a long sip of coffee and then said, "Pretty mysterious. Stay in Denver for a couple of days. I'll show you around."

She looked at her watch, set the fork on the plate next to the pancakes, half eaten, and said, "I need to get on the road."

"Already?"

She nodded, stood up and said, "Thanks for the breakfast. I'll save a place for you in my next life."

Teffinger grabbed her wrist and squeezed.

"I'd prefer this life."

4

Teffinger couldn't let her walk out of his life. More than that, though, he couldn't shake the feeling she was in some kind of trouble—the gun, the money, and now this mysterious meeting pulling her to Los Angeles, it was all pointing to a culmination of sorts; and last night, was that one last good meal before she got herself dead?

"Here's something crazy," he said. "I'll come with you."

"You'll come with me?"

"Sure, why not?"

She laughed.

"And then what?"

"Well, when we get there, I'll get on a plane and fly back, unless we decide between here and there that I shouldn't."

She got a distant look, teetered, and then shook her head.

"No, let it go."

"No?"

"No. It's not a good idea."

"That's where the really good things come from," he said. "The ones that start off as not-good ideas."

She tilted her head.

"Name one."

"I don't know—I'm just blowing smoke. One thing that is true, though, is that I know how to change a flat. Did I mention that?"

She smiled and pushed him away.

Then she got serious.

"What's your name again?"

"Nick."

She nodded.

"Right, I remember now—Nick, Nick Derringer."

"Teffinger, actually."

"You said Derringer last night."

That was true.

He remembered now.

"I do that sometimes."

"So one of the first things you told me was a lie?"

"Apparently so."

"Do you have a girlfriend?"

"No."

"A wife?"

"No."

"I don't need any more crazy bitches coming after me. So is that the truth or a lie?"

"The truth," he said. "The lies are all gone. I only have an arsenal of one, per person I mean."

She smiled.

"You should have saved it for something more important."

Her car wasn't much, in fact it wasn't even a car, it was a 30 or 40-year-old F-150 pickup, built back when all you could get was a single cab, never-babied, and with the scars and dents and scraps and cracked glass to prove it. Someone along the way had lifted it up 4 inches and stuck big old knobby off-road tires on; the front ones were worn at the edges from misalignment. It started life white but now the front fender was red and the hood was black and the rest, well, it still had a semblance of where it began life but had since morphed into another version of it. The interior was beat to death from whatever had been whooping at it and spilling on it all these years. Teffinger's first thought was that it would never make it to Los Angeles.

"Why don't we take my Tundra? It'll get us there."

"So will Thumper."

Teffinger held a hand to his ear as if listening and said, "Do you hear that? It's Thumper saying, *Pasture, give me a pasture. Any pasture. I don't care if it's green or not.*"

Jackie stuck her tongue out.

Then she tossed her suitcase in the bed and said, "You in or out?"

"In."

"Then let's go."

Inside, Jackie worked the clutch and the long-throw four on the floor as she pulled into traffic, not caring about the way her dress hiked up.

It was the sexiest thing Teffinger had ever seen.

They swung by his place for a quick suitcase, and he took the opportunity to duck to the side and call Sydney Heatherwood, the newbie of the homicide department, as Jackie made sandwiches and filled brown paper bags.

"Got a situation," he said. "I met a woman last night and I think she's in some kind of trouble. She's on her way to Los Angeles and I'm going to tag along."

"You're not coming in today?"

"No, I'm taking vacation days—I'll send HR an email. Here's the thing though; call me if anything serious comes up, or even if it's not serious. I'm at the other end of the line until I get back, is what I'm saying."

Sydney exhaled.

"Who's the woman?"

He told her—Jackie Jones, from Chicago.

He met her last night in a bar.

"What's the trouble she's in?"

"I don't know that she is yet," he said. "She's driving around in a pickup that isn't worth a broke-dick dog, but she's got twenty grand or more in cash in her purse, plus a Sig 9mm. She's headed to Los Angeles for some mysterious kind of meeting."

"Drugs," Sydney said.

"I don't think so."

"Okay, then she stole the money and is on the run."

"It's possible but it's not the feeling I get."

"Is the gun registered?"

"I don't know. She doesn't know I know about it. Same for the money."

"Do you want some advice?"

"No."

"Good, because here it is. Drop her, she's a criminal, and she doesn't sound like even a very good one at that. Whatever her game is, it doesn't matter. As far as saving her, even if you do, she'll get herself right back into something before you can poke your eyes out. I assume she's a curvy little thing—"

"She is."

"Too bad because you don't have a future with her, if that's what's driving you. Get back to work, we have bad guys to catch." A beat, then, "What were you doing in a bar last night to begin with?"

"It was the Blue Moon."

"That sleazebag on Colfax?"

"Right, except sleazebag's overly generous. Remember Janet Sandavol?"

"The name, vaguely—"

"Rumor was she might have harbored Rail Smith. She barkeeps at the Moon, so I thought I'd drop in and squeeze her a little."

"And that's where you met your little princess?"

"Right."

"In a lowlife, sleazy bar—"

"Right."

"Teff, are you even listening to yourself?"

5

They headed west on I-70 under a bright cerulean Colorado sky, putting Denver and the flatlands in their wake as the asphalt suddenly punched up, almost like a plane taking off, into ponderosa pines, rocky cliffs and mountain eye-candy at nature's best. Ordinarily Teffinger would be transfixed at how fast the mountains took hold but this time things were different. This time, he was next to Jackie Jones, whoever she was.

"Road trip," she said.

"Yeah."

"With benefits."

He smiled.

The windows were down, the tires and air were deafening, the turbulence in the cab was a force, and Teffinger wouldn't change an iota of it. Then, suddenly, just like that, he did something he didn't think he would, in fact, something he most definitely thought he wouldn't—he told her what he did.

"I sort of went in your purse this morning," he said. "I was just picking it up off the floor, not snooping or anything, but I saw what was inside—the gun and the money."

He shouldn't have said it.

He knew that the second the words came out and he realized he couldn't suck them back in and swallow them.

"You went in my purse?"

"Like I said, it was an accident."

She shook her head.

"You can't go into an envelope by accident. You have to pull it out and take rubber bands off. That's no accident."

"Okay, maybe at that point I was curious. The important thing is that I'm telling you because, like I said before, I only have one lie per person and I've already used mine up. I felt like not telling you was the equivalent of a lie."

She wasn't impressed.

"My purse is none of your business."

"I know that."

"Did I go in your wallet?"

"I'm assuming, no."

"That's right, no. You know why? Because you don't do that kind of thing to people you don't even know."

"I know."

"You know? It doesn't seem like you know."

"Look," he said, "I shouldn't have done it. But what's going on? Are you in some kind of trouble? Because if you are—"

"Stop talking."

She checked the rearview mirror, apparently saw no tailgaters, and pulled over to the shoulder where she brought the vehicle to a stop so suddenly that it lunged their faces towards the glass. A plume of dirt kicked up.

Then she stared at him.

He'd never seen eyes so cold.

"Out," she said.

"Look, I'm sorry—"

"Out!"

He scrambled for words, found none, and opened the door.

"Bye-bye, birdie," she said.

He stepped out.

Then the woman stuck her arm out the window, flipped him the bird and took off.

Teffinger stood there, dismissed, watching the rusty dented tailgate as it got smaller and smaller. A hundred yards off he'd had enough and gave her the finger to prove it.

"Bitch."

She stuck her arm back out the window and waved it, one finger flying high.

Then she was gone.

Traffic passed, not a lot, but a hundred percent by people who had no desire to stop and find out what a guy was doing out here at the side of I-70 all by himself.

Then his phone rang and Sydney's voice came through.

"Thought you'd find this interesting," she said. "Your princess, you might want to ask her what her real name is, because it's not Jackie Jones."

"What do you mean?"

"What I mean is, the state of Illinois has never issued a driver's license for a Jackie Jones from Chicago, or a Jacqueline Jones either, for that matter. Well, I'll take that back a bit; it has, but for a black woman, like you-know-who. I'm assuming your new princess isn't black."

"No, not exactly."

"Then she lied to you about her name; either that or lied

about being from Chicago."

"I saw her driver's license. It was Jackie Jones from Chicago."

"Then you saw a fake. Nick, do me a favor, let her go play her games. Get your posterior back to work where it belongs."

He considered it.

It was the right thing to do.

It was the smart thing to do.

"Can't do that," he said.

He hung up and stuck his thumb out.

"Damn I hate this woman."

6

No one picked him up. People stared as they drove past, and one woman even slowed down a little before she came to her senses. Then a Colorado State Patrol vehicle showed up.

"Teffinger?"

Teffinger recognized the face and voice but couldn't pull the name.

"Jake Walker," the man said. "I was the helicopter pilot the night you took down David Hallenbeck."

Teffinger remembered now — the storm, the lightning, the invisible black ground, somehow miraculously living to tell about it.

"Walker, right. What are you doing here?"

"Inner ear problem; lost my balance and ended up grounded."

"Ouch."

"Yeah, tell me about it."

Ten minutes later they were on the tail of an old F-150 pickup with the lights flashing and the siren blasting. The truck pulled over and Walker approached with a serious face.

"I have a man in the car back there by the name of Nick

Teffinger who says that you dumped him by the side of the road. Is that true?"

The woman, a blonde, said "Yes."

"That's a violation of wildlife laws," he said.

The woman screwed her face in puzzlement.

"I don't understand—"

"Do you know Teffinger?"

"A little."

"What do you think would happen to a bear if it stumbled on the guy and ate him?"

"I don't follow."

"It's a simple question, ma'am. A bear—meaning a protected wildlife species in Colorado—eats Teffinger, the person you dropped there. What do you think is going to happen to that bear? Do you think it's going to be pretty?"

"You mean for Teffinger?"

"No, for the bear. Have you ever eaten something so foul and poisonous that it could kill you?"

"No."

"So, you only eat things that are fit for consumption, is that right?"

"Yes."

"Well, answer me this. Do you think bears should have any less privileges?"

She pictured it.

"Probably not."

"Good, now we're getting somewhere. What I'm going to do, ma'am, is give you a chance to save a bear, and avoid a wildlife citation. I'm going to give you the chance to un-dump what you dumped out."

She turned and looked back.

Teffinger waved at her.

She told Walker, "You could get in trouble for this."

"Not really. We simply haven't gotten to the fun part yet, which is the part about you doing ten over the limit. Should we talk about that now or would you rather just forget it?"

"Let's just forget it."

He tipped his hat.

"In that case, have a nice day."

7

With Teffinger back in Thumper, Jackie wasn't amused. She popped the clutch directly into second with a power takeoff to prove it, and warned, "Don't get too comfy, I'm dropping you off the first chance I get. And tell me one thing—how did you get that cop to stop me?"

"We actually know each other. Our paths crossed once."

"How convenient."

She pulled her gun out of her purse and handed it to him. "See that green mile-marker coming up?"

He did.

"Shoot it when we go past."

"Why?"

"Because you went into my purse."

He almost said, *I can't shoot a weapon at random. It's illegal. I have fifty hours of training to the opposite.* Instead he said, "That's probably not a good idea."

"Do it or not, your choice, sailor."

The sign came up fast, too fast for Teffinger to get comfortable with breaking the law, but the consequences of not shooting made him pull the trigger at the last second. The bullet ripped through the metal with hardly a pause, leaving a hole big enough to see as it dashed past.

Jackie smiled.

Teffinger handed the weapon back and said, "We're cool now?"

She moved his hand to her knee.

"Yeah, we're cool."

They made their way up the divide, through the Eisenhower Tunnel, down the long dangerous decline on the western slope where the truckers did fifteen and the Porsches did a hundred, and then wound up and through and over and into more mountains and peaks and bursts of nature so compelling that nothing else existed. At Vail pass, they pulled in for the much-overdue facilities where, alone, Teffinger called Sydney with the Illinois license plate number of the pickup and said, "Find out who it's registered to. I got ten bucks on it being Jackie Jones."

"You're on, give me a few minutes."

Six minutes later she called back and said, "You owe me ten bucks."

"No way."

"I'm not going to forget about it either, Teffinger. You're going to pay this time."

"I always pay."

"True, if you define always as never. Take it out of your wallet and set it aside for me. Are you doing it?"

"Yes."

"No you're not. The vehicle's registered to a Chicago guy named Bernard Bee, as in the flying thing that stings. It's his truck. Luckily his phone's listed and I just got off the line with him. The story is, he had it for sale on Craigslist for $1500. A blond woman who never gave her name came over and bought it for cash on the condition that he leave the license plates on, which he did. He said the blondie looked like a movie star. He would have crawled over broken glass to give her the keys for free if she'd asked."

"I know the feeling."

"At least she didn't steal it," Sydney said.

"Did she say anything to him about why she wanted it?"

"I don't think so. He signed the title to her in blank without her name being filled in, and she asked if it had a name and he told her it did—Thumper—which she thought was cute."

"When did this happen?"

"Late Monday night. She probably wanted it for a crime."

"We don't know that."

"We do if we take the lust-goggles off. Take 'em off, Teffinger, that's my advice. Otherwise you're going to end up doing something stupider than usual and turn yourself into an accessory after the fact. Then you lose your job and I have to break in a new boss."

"You have me broken in?"

"Since we met, Teff, start paying attention. Hey, you still there?"

"Yeah."

"Do me a favor. Send me a selfie with your little princess in it. I want to see what you're throwing your life away for. Oh, and I almost forgot. As long as I was at the computer, I also checked to see if any Illinois plates were ever issued to a Jackie Jones. None were, which isn't surprising considering she doesn't exist."

8

Teffinger was a locomotive blasting down a track which was about go over a cliff. *Get ready for the drop, buddy boy.* Right now the drop wasn't in sight and he was enjoying the ride—the heat, the scenery, the tanned legs in the short dress, the way the woman held the clutch in her fingers. He wanted to believe that Jackie was a girl in trouble who needed saving. His detective mind, though, kept dragging the facts back into the mix, and the more he looked at them, the more his eyes burned.

Accessory after the fact.

Those were words he needed to avoid.

Being wrong about the woman was one thing. Crossing the line was a whole something else.

"Can I see your gun again?" he said.

The words weren't what Jackie expected and she put an expression on her face to prove it, then nodded in amusement and said, "Sure."

He took it out of the purse, waited for clear spot with no other cars around, and shot a ponderosa pine in the trunk.

Jackie grinned.

"Feel good?"

"Actually, yes," he said. What he didn't say is that he now had a bullet for forensics, if he ever needed it.

"You're a little wilder than you look," she said.

"Is that a compliment?"

"An observation. So what's the craziest thing you've ever done?"

He chewed on it.

"I've only ever told this to one person, and did it only because she made me."

"She made you?"

"Yes."

"How?"

"She told me to tell her something that I'd never told any-one before. Then she'd do the same."

"So you swapped secrets."

"Exactly."

Jackie smiled.

"Are you glad you did it?"

"Yes."

"Tell you what," Jackie said. "I'll play."

"You mean, swap?"

She nodded.

"First tell me what you told her because my curiosity's up at this point. But it won't count as a secret because you've already told someone. You'd have to tell me something else after it. Something you've never told anybody; something that only me and you will know."

"And you'll do the same?"

"Yes."

"It has to be something good, though," Teffinger said. "It can't be something lame, especially since you're basically getting two for one."

She extended her hand to shake.

"My secrets are a lot of things but lame isn't one of them," she said. "Now, start flapping those little kissy lips of yours."

He leaned over.

"Let me use the kissy part first."

She obliged.

He took two, as long as he was there.

Then he cleared his throat. "You probably never heard of the Denver news reporter from Channel 8, Jenna Lake."

"No."

"Well, she and I went to school together back in Fort Collins, which is up in northern Colorado. One of our friends had a farm, and his dad had a bunch of wild animals, including a black panther."

"As in, the thing from Africa?"

Teffinger nodded. "It had been born in captivity and hand-fed and all that since it was a little cub, so it was pretty friendly."

"Still—"

"Exactly," Teffinger said. "Still, it was carrying around all those crazy little genetics. We used to go in the cage with it and sit for a half hour or so—all three of us. Then one day when we were in there, Billy dared me to spend a whole night in the cage, with the full darkness and all, all the way until dawn. Before I knew what I was doing, I said, 'Sure, I'll do it if Jenna will,' because I knew she wouldn't and then I'd have an out. But then she said, 'Yeah, okay, why not?'"

Jackie pictured it.

"How old were you?"

"I was in high school, Jenna was three years behind us, in junior high."

"So she was younger—"

"Three years younger, but even so, I had a crush on her like you couldn't believe. To this day I've still never felt like that again."

"Did she ever find out?"

"Not for a long time, we went different ways and all that, but when she came to Denver for the TV gig we ended up hooking up, nothing serious, but with benefits. Anyway, we showed up around dusk to spend the night in the cage. Billy didn't join us, he was the sane one—it was just me and Jenna. The first hour or so was fine, then after full dark came, the panther started pacing back and forth and getting real agitated, as if he didn't want anyone in his territory anymore. Jenna wanted out and to be honest, so did I. What happened, though, was that I dropped the key outside to the ground when I went to open the lock. Jenna freaked out and curled up behind me and held on tight and didn't let go, not for hours. I'm sure we dozed off a few times now and then but basically we just held onto each other until morning. Then Billy came and got the lock off."

"Cool."

"Yeah, but that's not the secret," Teffinger said. "The secret is, I had a second key in my pocket the whole time. I was actually reaching for it after I dropped the first key, but the way Jenna grabbed onto me, well, I froze. It was one of those moments I'd been thinking about for a long, long time."

"Did you ever tell her?"

"No."

"So she doesn't know, even to this day?"

"No, I've kept it a secret. And now it's your duty to keep it the same way."

"I will."

He grinned and said, "Jenna never went back in that cage again."

"How about you?"

"I almost did, to prove that I could, but it never quite happened. Your turn—"

"Yeah, fine, but just for the record, that wasn't very nice, putting that girl in danger just so you could get a squeeze. I mean, you didn't know what that animal would do. It could have snapped."

"I didn't do it just to get a squeeze. I did it so she'd have a story to tell for the rest of her life. Me too, for that matter. Your turn."

9

"My turn, huh?" Jackie said.

"Yes."

"Okay, let me think. I was on a road trip once going through Utah with my older cousin; I was sixteen at the time, she was nineteen. We were out in the middle of nowhere and I had to use the facilities. So, with no one being around, I slipped out of my dress and stepped over by a bush to do what I had to do. My cousin was supposed to be watching for cars. Anyway, that didn't happen, because this car came from out of nowhere barreling around the turn. A guy was driving and he saw me, got seriously distracted, and drove right over a cliff. Boom, he was there; and then boom, he was gone."

"You're kidding."

"Killed him," she said. "We climbed down to check on him and he was a bloody dead mess—the first person I ever saw dead, for the record. He didn't need his money anymore, so we took that. Then we checked in the trunk. We found something in there that turned out to be something on the special side."

"Like what?"

She studied him, deciding, and then said, "A painting by Monet, a real one, not a copy or fake or anything like that. It had been stolen out of a museum twenty years earlier."

"So what'd you do with it?"

"Sold it," she said.

"That'd be impossible," Teffinger said. "There are federal registries that tag stolen art."

"Trust me, it's not impossible, it's not impossible at all," she said. "But I will tell you one thing. I had to keep it hidden for five years while I figured out how to do it."

"So who'd you sell it to?"

"That's something I can't divulge."

"Someone in the United States?"

She chuckled at the thought.

"No."

Teffinger cocked his head.

"You're putting me on, right?"

She shook her head.

"Life's funny, huh?"

Criminal.

That's the word that ricocheted through Teffinger's gray matter as the miles and miles of rocky mountain terrain clicked off and the wind whistled in his ears and the sun beat down on the cab. Sydney was right; he needed to stop throwing good time after bad and get back to Denver. This woman—this little Jackie—as hypnotic as she was, wasn't built for him. She was built for someone else, someone on the other side of the line. Every ounce of reason told him to get out at the next gas station. Still, they passed one, then another, and he kept the seat filled.

Hey, you're a crazy bitch
But you fuck me so good, I'm on top of it
When I dream, I'm doing you all night

He didn't know who sang that song, and hadn't heard it that many times, only at clubs, but he suddenly understood it the way it needed to be understood.

Past Vail they were greeted by lower, less-winding, more-open terrain, punctuated with rusty bluffs, farther horizon lines, railroad tracks, telephone poles and a more southwest patina.

At a gas stop, he called Sydney who told him, "I've been sniffing around in Chicago to see if I could figure out what your little princess is running away from . . ."

"Nothing."

"You might be right," Sydney said, "but here's something to chew on. A lawyer got murdered three days ago, a guy by the name of Grayson Everly."

"And?"

"And, the detective in charge is a guy named Vic Vine, who I just spoke to. As far as he can tell, nothing was going on in the lawyer's life out of the ordinary except for one thing—he may or may not have been having an affair."

"That's pretty vague."

"That's because it is. The suggestion came from one of the guy's co-workers, based on nothing more than a feeling, as in, the victim never specifically mentioned a woman or said anything to that effect."

"How about the wife?"

"According to Vine, the wife said her husband was as true-blue as a 50's love song. She couldn't even imagine him doing anything he shouldn't."

"The wife would know."

"Or more likely, be the last to know," Sydney said. "The timing's right, the lawyer getting murdered and your little princess beating feet in a Craigslist car, both around the same time. What's waiting for her in Los Angeles? Someone who's going to get her to a county where they don't have extradition?"

"Talk about thin," Teffinger said.

"Thin or thick, there it is," Sydney said.

"Okay, let me ask you this," Teffinger said. "Assume she was having an affair with him, why would she murder him?"

"I don't know."

"Was anything taken?"

"Nothing apparent, yet."

"Is any money missing from his bank accounts?"

"No, no money or anything like that."

"No credit card statements for jewelry or hotels or unexplained dinners?"

"No, cheaters use cash."

Teffinger shook his head.

"I have to be honest," he said. "I don't see the makings of an affair, or a motive to kill him if there was one—unless you're talking about the wife killing him and then pretending everything was hunky-dory."

"Just be careful," Sydney said. "I'm texting you Vine's contact information if you want to call him."

"I don't."

"Teffinger, you can get a million women. Why are you locking yourself into the absolute worst one you can find, not to mention abandoning your job? You're making zero sense."

He smiled.

"That's better than my normal sense, which is negative one. How did the lawyer die?"

"His throat was slit," Sydney said. "An act of passion, something a mistress would do."

"Or a wife."

"Oh, one other strange thing," Sydney said. "Something was carved on the lawyer's chest. Some kind of picture."

"A picture of what?"

"I don't know, the outline of a woman or something like that."

"Have you seen it?"

"No, Vine just told me about it."

"Get the image and forward it to me."

"Why?"

"I had a case like that once. I want to see if there's a match."

10

Teffinger didn't want to do it, not at all; but he got an innocent selfie of himself with Jackie, edited himself out, and emailed what was left to Sydney so she could forward it to the detective, Vine, who could show it around to the dead lawyer's friends and whatnot to see if anyone recognized her.

He felt dirty.

He was going behind her back.

That was nothing more than a form of lying straight to her face.

The whole thing made his chest pound. Someone may in fact recognize her. *Yeah, I've seen that woman before, I bumped into Grayson at lunch one day way down on the south side—hell, I don't know, a month ago, maybe?—and she was with him. A real looker, that one. Not your average client, although they do occasionally come packaged like that, just not that often.*

Then what would he do?

Sydney called back, "I can see why you're gaga. I'd do her myself."

"Fine, I'll watch."

"Sorry, dude. If you're in the room, you need to be working. With me, there are no passengers, only crew."

The road swept into a descending twisty canyon with slow curves in front of them, steep rocky crags to their left and the muddy-brown waters of the Colorado River to their right. The river forced greenery at its sides, trying to be a picture-perfect oasis in an arid setting and coming pretty damn close.

Then the road entered Grand Junction where it ran flat and crowded and not very aspiring, at least not from this angle.

"There's a McDonald's coming up," Jackie said. "You want to feed me?"

"I do. You want something better?"

"There is nothing better when you're on the road. Hell, I've gone on the road just to justify stopping there."

Teffinger smiled.

They gassed up.

They got junk food to go.

Then they were back on the road, entering a desolate arid topography of wind-worn treeless mountains and hot, sizzling rocks. Half an hour into the drive, a service road appeared on their right. To Teffinger's surprise, Jackie pulled off onto it, came to a stop and said, "Get out."

"Why?"

"I have to make a run."

"To where?"

"To somewhere. I'll be back, don't worry."

"This is a little weird—"

"Yeah, maybe," she said. "Keep an eye out for rattlesnakes."

He stepped out into the thick sweltering sun with a half-empty plastic cup of diet Pepsi in his left hand and watched as Thumper snaked up the dirt road into the desolate gray mountains and disappeared. Two large black birds circled high above him on silent wings.

He looked up and said, "Not today, buddy."

On his phone, a new email from Sydney had an attached image of the carving in the lawyer's chest. It crudely resembled the outline of a woman's body, sitting in sort of a curled up position. It resembled his prior case in that it was a carving, but not in any other way.

Thirty minutes later Thumper reappeared and came to a stop, kicking up a plume of dust.

Teffinger leaned against the driver's door and said, "Where'd you go?"

"I dumped the gun," she said.

"Why?"

"Because it's not registered and can only get me in trouble," she said. "Plus, I don't need it anymore. I have you to protect me."

"Protect you from what?"

"You never know."

Walking around the back, Teffinger noticed something in Thumper's bed next to his suitcase, namely a small wooden box that hadn't been there before, looking as it if had been underground for years and just now got dug up.

He got in, closed the door and said, "Looks like we have a new friend back there."

Jackie hardened her eyes.

"Don't ever go in it," she said.

"Why not?"

She turned off the engine and stared straight ahead. Then she locked eyes with him and said, "You need to promise me."

He shrugged.

"Sure."

"Yeah?"

"Yeah."

"You promise?"

"I do."

"Good. I was afraid I was going to have to leave you here." She smiled. "I can't wait for the sun to go down. I'm done with this heat."

11

The relentless sizzle of the sun dialed back ever so slightly as the shadows grew longer and the colors got richer. The traffic all but disappeared and the vistas popped up in all directions. They were heading through remote, high-prairie desert now, mostly on a straight road periodically interrupted by long sweeping curves. Long-distance canyons appeared and vanished, most of which probably hadn't been visited by man in decades. A sandy-rust color dominated, dotted with viridian green brush, as if strategically laid in by an artist's hand. A low thunderstorm thirty miles or more to their right threw the ground below it into a tease of moisture. It wouldn't happen. Whatever rain fell would get sucked to bone before it hit the ground.

Jackie skirted to the left edge of her lane to avoid squashing a rattlesnake slithering across the asphalt.

"Most people would have gone for it," Teffinger said.

"It's payback."

Teffinger wrinkled his face.

"One saved my life once," Jackie said.

"A rattlesnake saved your life?"

"Yeah, true story."

"How?"

"It came up out of nowhere and bit a guy just when he needed to be bit," she said. "It was almost like some kind of divine intervention."

"What was the guy doing?"

"When he got bit? Actually, he was pulling down his pants. It bit him right on the dick."

"No way."

Jackie nodded. "True story."

Teffinger smiled and said, "It reminds me of that old Lone Ranger joke. Have you ever heard it?"

"I don't think so."

"Okay, well, the Lone Ranger and Tonto were out in the desert and the Lone Ranger stops to take a leak and a rattlesnake jumps up and bites him on the dick, which almost immediately starts to swell. *Go get a doctor!* he tells Tonto. So Tonto jumps on his horse and hightails it into town. There, the doctor is with a woman who's about to give birth. He can't leave but he tells Tonto what to do. He says, *Make a small incision where the bite is and suck the venom out.* Tonto gets back on his horse and heads back to the Lone Ranger who now is in an even worse world of hurt and asks, *Where's the doctor?* Tonto says, *He can't come.* And the Lone Ranger says, *Well did you talk to him?* Tonto says, *Yes.* And the Lone Ranger says, *Well, what'd he say?* And Tonto shook his head and said, *He said you're going to die.*"

Jackie laughed.

"*He said you're going to die.* Good one."

A sign came up.

Green River – 10 miles.

Next Services – 107 miles.

"Green River, Utah," Jackie said. "It's not exactly Paris,

I'm guessing."

"Have you ever been there? To Paris?"

Jackie nodded.

"Many times. The Louvre is my favorite place in the world."

Green River, Utah, wasn't right on the interstate, in fact, it was a good fives miles north to town, which turned out to be an eclectic mix of traveler services and a small permanent population. They got a cheap room in a one-story hotel that reminded Teffinger of the one from *Psycho*. They showered and changed, ate like kings at a small wooden restaurant called The Kitchen, replete with homemade cherry pie, and then took two bottles of Lindeman's red wine down to a reclusive spot on the river, which actually existed and actually was green.

Twilight was thick. Full darkness was on the way.

Stars were starting to appear as faint white specs.

Teffinger felt good; perfect, actually—but he couldn't get the wooden box out of his gray matter. Strangely, Jackie hadn't brought it into the room earlier; she'd left it in the bed of Thumper, as if it were trash.

Tomorrow, that's when he'd think about it.

Right now it was just noise.

Jackie leaned back flat, stretched her arms up over her head and said, "The stars are starting to come out."

"Yeah."

She wiggled her body and said, "I want to remember tonight forever."

Teffinger straddled her chest and pinned her arms in place, then gave her a teasing kiss, pulling back as she responded.

"If you're serious, I can make that happen," he said.

"Then go for it, sailor."

53

DAY TWO

July 8
Thursday

12

The next morning while Jackie was in the shower, Teffinger stepped outside and called Sydney to see if the selfie had generated any hits as to Jackie being the maybe-yes and maybe-no mistress of the definitely-dead Chicago lawyer, Grayson Everly.

"No," Sydney said. "In fact, ironically, I just got off the phone with Vine. No one recognizes your little buttercup. Vine has shown the photo at every restaurant that the lawyer used a credit card at in the last two months. No one remembers ever seeing her."

Teffinger smiled.

"That's good."

"Are you smiling?"

"I am."

"Then wipe it off because the rest of the news isn't as pretty," she said. "I asked Leigh Sandt if she'd run a facial recognition. She did and it turns out that your little princess, Jackie Jones—her real name is Jacqueline Angelica."

"Okay."

"No, not okay, not okay at all. She's an international fugitive. She's got arrest warrants out for her in cases coming out of Paris, Rome, Shanghai and Tokyo, to name a few."

He swallowed.

"What kind of cases?"

"Black market, basically. High value black market, to be even more precise," Sydney said. "Paintings, artifacts, you name it. If half of her reputation is true, she's got a network in place to move just about anything. Have you stolen something from the Louvre lately? Then give her a call, she has a buyer for it."

"Damn."

"Interestingly, no one knows much about her. She grew up in Los Angeles; her parents died early on and she basically got raised by an older cousin; she went to Berkley, sang in a local blues group at night, and dropped out in her senior year. Then she largely disappeared from the radar screen."

"In what way?"

"In every way," Sydney said. "There's no trace of her after that, at least not under the name Jacqueline Angelica. There are no credit cards, no bank accounts, no tax returns—no nothing. No doubt that's when she got into the black market stuff—she would have been about twenty or twenty-one at the time. Now she's twenty-eight."

Teffinger's stomach churned.

"Has Leigh contacted any of these countries?"

"No. She wants to know what you're up to first."

"Do me a favor and keep her quiet for a day or two.."

"While you do what?"

"I don't know. Figure things out—"

"Teff, are you even listening to yourself?"

"I stopped doing that years ago."

"Lucky you. I wish I'd done the same. Cut your loses and get back to Denver. I'm getting tired of having to say it."

Hanging up, Teffinger's chest tightened and his fingers twitched.

Jackie had to have money, lots and lots of the stuff, so there wasn't any good explanation for why she was driving around in a broke-dick dog like Thumper, except to be laying low. Was one of the countries closing in on her?

Sydney had a point—why get involved?

What kind of future could he possibly have with the woman? She was a criminal, the exact opposite of everything he stood for, which would have to become a divider sooner or later. And now, worse, she was a criminal on the run. What was he going to do, run with her for the rest of his life?

She was dirty.

How long could he possibly be around her without getting that same dirt in his lungs and in his eyes and in every pore of his skin to the point where he couldn't stand it one second longer?

He stepped back in the room just as the woman was coming out of the shower.

Her eyes looked into his, way into his.

Whatever it was that she saw, it made her smile, ever so slightly, almost child-like.

At that second, he knew—letting the world pounce on her wasn't an option, even if she'd invited the pounce.

He couldn't let her get hurt.

He couldn't ever see pain in those eyes.

She walked to him, put her arms around his neck and whispered in his ear, "Merci pendant la nuit derniere. Do you know what I just said?"

"No. I didn't know you spoke French."

"There are a few things about me you don't know yet."

"I'm guessing it's more than a few. So what'd you say?"

"I said . . . oh, forget it. It was stupid."

"What was stupid?"

"Nothing."

She pulled the window curtain to the side, peeked out, nodded her head towards a black Mercedes sedan across the road and down a hundred yards and said, "That's the second time I've seen that car this morning."

Teffinger focused on it.

Two figures were inside.

Their faces were indistinguishable, nothing more than silhouettes at this distance.

"Friends of yours?"

Jackie tightened her brow.

"That can't be. But it's weird."

"Well, let's find out."

Teffinger opened the door with a force and walked briskly towards the sedan. He didn't get more than ten steps before the vehicle started up and wisked off in the opposite direction.

Back at Jackie, Teffinger said, "Who were they?"

"I don't know."

Teffinger frowned.

"I can't help you if you won't cooperate."

"There's nothing to help me with."

He shook his head.

"We both know that's not true."

She exhaled and said, "Do me a favor. Go outside and get that box out of the back of Thumper."

13

She examined the wooden box when Teffinger brought it in, must have found it to her satisfaction, and said, "You passed your test, you didn't tamper with it. I'm impressed. Go ahead and open it if you want."

He obliged.

The wood was weak and the nails were rusty but it was still a bit of work to tear it open with his bare hands. Inside was a yellow waterproof case.

"Keep going," Jackie said.

He released the latches and lifted the top.

Inside was a human skull.

It was covered in detailed red markings.

"That was my boyfriend, before you," Jackie said. "He asked too many questions." Teffinger must have had a look because the woman broke into laughter and said, "Relax, I'm just messing with you."

"So what is it?"

"Not someone I killed, if that's what you're thinking,"

she said. "He's an old Egyptian guy. The markings are a map, if the story's true."

"A map to what?"

"Unknown."

With that, she pulled out her cell phone and photographed the skull from every angle, checking to make sure every mark was clearly recorded. Then she emailed them to some-one—maybe herself.

"I bought it off a guy back when I was twenty-two," she said. "We were doing some business and it was sitting on the end of an old wooden bench. He didn't know much about it other than what I just told you. I asked him what he wanted for it and he said a hundred dollars, so I figured what the hell. I buried it here for safekeeping while I was passing through town—when was that, six years ago, I guess. I was hoping I'd come across more information as the years went on but that hasn't happened. So far, all I've done is waste a hundred dollars."

"So why are you digging it up now?"

"Because I'm in the area so why not? At least I have pho-tos of it now. My memory was worth nothing."

They checked out, with no black Mercedes in sight. Half an hour later Jackie's eyes fell to the rearview mirror and her face got serious.

"We got a black car behind us."

Teffinger turned.

The vehicle was a long ways back but was definitely dark.

His eyes couldn't tell if it was the Mercedes or not but his gut could.

They were being followed.

14

The black vehicle hung back a respectable distance for the next ten miles of barren desert highway and then suddenly accelerated hard, doing at least a hundred to Thumper's seventy.

"They're coming!" Jackie said.

The gap closed fast.

The passenger, a muscular male with a chiseled face, leaned out the window and fired a warning shot into the air.

"What do we do?"

"Keep going—"

The gun fired again and a bullet ripped into the tailgate.

"Shit!"

Another shot came, exploding the taillight, followed quickly by another that shattered the glass behind their heads with a sound so powerful and deafening that Teffinger's entire body twitched.

"Get off the road!" he said.

Jackie jerked the wheel and Thumper twisted violently to the right, almost going up on two wheels as it left the road and shot wildly into the hostile desert terrain. The front end bounced off something, shot up high and crashed down with a serious force.

"Keep it straight!" Teffinger yelled.

Jackie did, very well in fact, avoiding a full tip or flip, but couldn't avoid a trench that grabbed the front end like the devil himself and jerked everything to a whiplashing halt. She jammed the clutch into reverse and gunned it only to have the back tires spin. They were two hundred yards off the road.

"Come on!"

They got out and ran.

The Mercedes was stopped on the road, unable to follow, but the two men were already out and running after them with guns in hand.

A shot fired.

The dirt to their right kicked up with an explosion.

"Shit!" Teffinger said.

"I can't breathe!"

"Don't stop!"

The sun was on them with every ounce of fury it had.

The air was an oven.

They ran for a hundred yards, then another. The men didn't fall behind but couldn't close the gap either and eventually stopped and fired until their bullets ran out. Teffinger and Jackie kept going, but at a slower, more human pace. Eventually they stopped, fell to the ground in the shade of a rabbit bush and collapsed on their backs as the sweat from their bodies ran into the dirt.

They were alive.

Nothing else mattered.

15

So who are your two friends?" Teffinger said.

"I don't know."

"Come on."

Jackie exhaled.

"I'm not exactly sure, but they could be related to a transaction I was involved in last year that went bad."

"What kind of transaction?"

She looked into his eyes and said, "You can't ever tell anybody, if I tell you."

"Fine."

"You promise?"

"It's going to my grave. Now tell me what it is that I'm taking there."

She studied him, apparently found no lies and said, "I do a little bit of work in the black market, paintings and artifacts and whatever, finding buyers for sellers, sellers for buyers, arranging and overseeing the transactions. Last year I set one up. A Frenchman—a guy by the name of Boudiette—had a pretty nice stolen Van Gogh he wanted to get rid of. I arranged a sale of it to a middle-eastern man for a sum that would be roughly equivalent to ten million dollars. I had the painting in my possession to do the transaction and someone stole it from me. I don't know who."

"The buyer?"

"I doubt it," she said. "He wasn't that sophisticated. In any event, the deal obviously didn't go through and I didn't have the Van Gogh to return to Boudiette, or the money from the sale since it didn't go through, so I was stuck."

"What'd you do?"

"The only thing I could do—I went into hiding, from him at least, not from everyone, obviously," she said. "My guess is that somehow he's caught up to me."

"To kill you," Teffinger said.

"Maybe, but that wouldn't be his first choice," she said. "His first choice would be to get the money out of me, at least the ten million. It's been a year. He knows full well I would have made that much by now."

Teffinger raised an eyebrow.

"Have you?"

"Yes," she said. "I have that much and more in a Cayman account."

Teffinger shrugged.

"So pay him."

"It's not that easy," she said. "Personally, I never viewed myself as a guarantor of results. Things could go wrong. The risk of that happening was on him, not me."

"But that's not how he views it."

"He thinks I stole the painting and then fabricated a story that someone else did it. He thinks I played him."

"Did you?"

"Absolutely not. It happened just like I told you—someone else stole it from me." She shook her head. "God, I was hoping this was behind me. I haven't spoken to him since it happened and now, wham!—he's back. I don't know why. I'm sure the whole thing hurt financially speaking, but it wasn't fatal, not by a long shot. It was more like a flesh wound." She exhaled and added, "Everything that happened today, I can't have the police involved. You can't make a report or anything like that. Tell me I can trust you."

Teffinger didn't hesitate.

"You can trust me."

They waited a good hour in the heat before carefully circling back to Thumper. Jackie's purse was dumped out; the money, as well as her wallet and cell phone, were all gone. Their suitcases were on the ground, ripped opened, with the contents strewn about. The keys were gone from the ignition. Teffinger's cell phone, which had been on the seat, was gone.

"Hold on," Jackie said. "The guy who sold me this car told me something."

She fished around under the front bumper and retrieved a key attached to a tie rod with electrical tape. It actually fit into the ignition like it should and equally turned to the right. The vehicle started.

"No song ever sounded that good," Teffinger said.

"Amen."

"Well, maybe Brown Eyed Girl, but that would be it."

Jackie sang,

> *Making love in the green grass*
> *Behind the stadium with you,*
> *Brown eyed girl,*
> *You my brown eyed girl.*

"You're pretty good," Teffinger said.

"I was in a band once."

"Seriously?"

"Yeah. We never went anywhere."

They got the vehicle in four-wheel-drive and, with a lot of effort and finagling, managed to rock it loose and get back to the highway, where the Mercedes was long gone.

Back on the road, the front wheel wobbled hard starting at about fifty, so they kept it just under that. Five miles into it, Teffinger felt around under the front seat to see if by chance his cell phone had fallen there.

It hadn't but Jackie's had.

He shoved it back under and stole a glance at Jackie to see if she'd noticed, which she hadn't.

I haven't spoken to him since it happened and now, wham!— he's back. Of all the things Jackie said, that was the most important.

The dogs may or may not belong to Boudiette.

To a point, it was irrelevant.

Jackie didn't suddenly buy a wimp-dick truck last week and shoot across the country incognito because of something that happened a year ago.

No, whatever she was on the run from, it wasn't Boudiette.

It was something that happened recently or, at a minimum, something from the past that caught up with her recently, something that she knew had caught up with her.

That wasn't Boudiette.

Boudiette might be a secondary problem but he wasn't the primary one.

"You're thinking," Jackie said.

Teffinger tightened his brow.

"I've never done that before."

"Done what?"

"Run."

She patted his knee.

"It feels like a cheap suit," he added.

She said, "You've heard the saying, *Never bring a knife to a gun fight?* That goes double for fists."

"Yeah, I know, but still—"

She smiled.

"With Thumper stuck at fifty, relax, because you're probably going to get a re-do." She got serious and said, "I should have kept that gun. Maybe we should go back and get it."

Teffinger chewed on the idea and the more he did, the better it tasted.

"Let's do it," he said.

"Are you serious?"

"Dead. Turn this Thump-machine around."

16

At a roadside rest area, Teffinger snuck Jackie's cell phone into the men's room and fired it up. A low battery warning filled the screen. He clicked it off and opened Contacts which was filled with hundreds of names and numbers, most international.

He scrolled down.

Damn it.

Damn it to hell.

The dead lawyer, Grayson Everly, was there on the list, large as life, with three phone numbers listed. One must be his office and the other his cell. What was the third one, a secret cell phone exclusive to only him and Jackie?

Teffinger's chest tightened.

He checked the phone records to see if she had called any of the dead lawyer's numbers, only to find the history deleted.

Then he checked the Google history and found the woman had done a lot of research on a man named John Winterfield, an American who apparently ended up in a Thai prison. She'd also done a lot of research on a Cezanne painting that had been stolen from an English museum way back in 1999.

The men's room door opened.

"Nick, did you die in there or what?"

He powered off.

"On my way."

When he came out, Jackie rubbed her stomach against his and said, "I missed you."

He kissed her and said, "Let's get that gun."

She nodded towards a public phone.

"Let me use your credit card for a minute," she said.

"Why?"

"I'm going to call my phone and see if anyone answers."

Teffinger swallowed, handed her his wallet and headed for Thumper, saying, "Give it a try. I got to change my shirt."

He made sure Jackie wasn't looking and tossed the phone through the window onto the seat, never opening the door, then got a fresh shirt out of his suitcase and slipped it on as he walked back.

The phone rang.

"Did you hear that?" he said.

"No, hear what?"

"Hold on."

He walked to the car, opened the door, grabbed the phone and reached under the front seat, as if he was finding it there. Then he waved it over his head as if he'd found King Tut's tomb.

"Bingo!"

Her face lit up.

He checked for his phone in the same place, in every crack and crevice under the seat, and didn't find it. They dialed his number from Jackie's phone and got no answer.

Then they were back on the road, with Teffinger driving and Jackie checking her phone. If she'd somehow found that it had been recently accessed, she kept it off her face.

He was as sure as he could be, without having actually been in the room with them, that Jackie was the dead lawyer's mysterious mistress, but couldn't think of why she'd kill him.

That didn't necessarily give him comfort.

Motives were tricky.

They could suddenly materialize, just like that, from where there had been nothing but an empty void before. Maybe the lawyer had promised Jackie something and then didn't deliver; used her, in effect—rode her hard and put her away wet. Maybe he'd gotten rough with her. Maybe he found out something about her—something about her black market dealings, for example—and threatened to disclose her, unless she did something for him, something illegal, something that he needed done and didn't dare do himself. So, she killed him and then left a carving on his chest to make it look like some maniac got him.

Speculation, it was all speculation.

He flicked his eyes into the rearview mirror constantly, on the lookout for the black Mercedes. So far it hadn't shown its ugly face. Maybe the two assholes had given up whatever it was they were doing and pissed back to where they came from.

It was possible.

Teffinger doubted it, though.

They were out there, circling.

He could feel it down in his blood.

"We're getting close," Jackie said.

That was true.

Thirty minutes later they crossed the highway, took one last look to be sure the black Mercedes wasn't around, and kicked up a plume of dust as they twisted into the hills.

"It's about a mile down," Jackie said.

The desolation was palpable.

The air was fire.

No trees grew, not a one.

Ground vegetation was almost non-existent.

Nothing wanted to learn how to live here.

The hills got steeper.

The road narrowed and got less and less recognizable as such. It didn't turn and try to circle out. It kept winding deeper and deeper. At some point there would be an end as dead as a dead end could be.

Suddenly the rear tire exploded.

17

The explosion turned out to be a violent protest of the tire against the heat and the rocks and the weight and the sun and the endless miles of use and abuse that had worn it to a final state of exhaustion. It had given up. It had had enough. It was out of here. *Bye-bye, Thumper—see you in hell.*

Jackie said, "I hope you weren't kidding when you said you could change one of those."

"Apparently we're going to find out."

The lug nuts were stubborn, the jack was rusty, the vehicle was tilted and the spare had only half its air, but Teffinger worked at it and worked at it, all under an inferno cloudless sky that barred down with an unrelenting stranglehold.

Three large black birds circled overhead, not high on a wind current, but low, as if supper was about to be served on the ground.

Jackie sat on a boulder in the shade, watching, then slipped off down the road and made a phone call.

Half an hour after he started, Teffinger muscled the flat into the bed, flipped up the tailgate and said, "You could die out here real easy."

He was a mess—dirty, rusty and drenched in sweat; and poured water over his head to prove it.

Jackie walked over, gave him a peck on the lips and said, "That was the sexiest thing I've ever seen."

Teffinger dried his face with his shirt and said, "You need to get out more."

Then they were back in motion.

Two minutes later, lodged in a crevice behind a boulder, they retrieved the Sig and box of bullets.

The turnaround wasn't pretty, and Thumper had to kiss a few boulders, but it got done. Then suddenly, not more than a hundred yards on the way out, a gunshot erupted, barely perceptible over the noise of Thumper's engine and the protesting of its tires against the rocks, but perceptible nonetheless. Teffinger snapped the vehicle to a stop.

His chest pounded

No one was in sight in any direction.

A motion caught his eye, something incredibly fast, coming from the sky. A large black bird hit the hood with the force of a sledgehammer, bounced violently, and came back down in its own dent.

A bloody stump showed where its head should be.

"What the fuck?"

Teffinger got the Sig in hand, rapidly checked the terrain behind the vehicle to be sure no one was back there, and found it empty, as it should be and as he expected. Then he got Jackie out, pushed her that way and said, "Find a place to hide and stay there."

"Nick—"

"Do it!"

His breath was tight but not all was lost. He had the Sig and would use it if he had to. More importantly, it didn't smell like an ambush. The Mercedes guys had handguns; it would have been hard to hit a bird with one of those; that more likely came a rifle. Plus, if someone were there to kill Jackie, why would they announce it by taking out a bird? With any luck the whole situation was nothing more that a couple of teenagers with rifles out getting their giggles by killing whatever they could get in their scopes.

He proceeded up the road, one silent step at a time, zigzagging his eyes for even the slightest movement.

A quick look behind showed no Jackie, which was good.

The other two birds continued to circle in the same spot that their buddy had just been blown out of.

A strange thought descended.

Maybe it was an ambush after all.

Maybe Jackie was being tracked through her cell phone. Maybe the Mercedes guys left the phone behind on purpose.

Still, even with that, why kill the bird?

He continued on with forward motion.

Fifty yards passed, then a hundred.

Nothing happened.

Then, as he came around a bend, he saw a black Mercedes in the narrow of the road a quarter-mile or so up ahead. By its diagonal angle, it was either stuck or parked like that on purpose. Either way, it was blocking the road.

Teffinger ducked behind a boulder and stole what glances he could.

There was no sign of either man.

Where the hell were they?

His blood raced.

Don't panic.

Keep your cool.

He moved forward with extreme caution. Then he realized that the bird couldn't have been shot from anywhere around here. It had to be back by Thumper. The guys must have found a good hiding place and let Teffinger pass right on by.

He shot out two of the vehicle's tires.

Then he turned back and ran.

Jackie!

Hold on, baby!

Hold on!

Hold on!

18

Teffinger hadn't gone more than fifty yards when a gunshot erupted from above and a bullet flew past his face so close that his hair sucked into the vacuum. The shooter was on the side of the hill tucked behind a grouping of boulders. Teffinger dived for cover, landing on his chest with a force that slapped the air out of his lungs, then rolled wildly towards the hill. The shooter no longer had a direct line of sight to him, but there was nowhere to go.

He was pinned in.

He worked at getting his breath back, gun in hand and ready to pull the trigger at the first chance.

Seconds passed, then more, then maybe even a full minute.

No shots came from above.

The guy didn't come into sight.

He could be maneuvering to get an angle.

The silence was deafening.

The only sound Teffinger could hear was the pumping of his own blood inside his ears.

He got to his feet in a crouching position, scanning one way, then the other, then up, for the first sign of movement.

He'd fire immediately, if for no other reason than to let the guy know this wasn't one-sided like the last time. Maybe deep down the guy was a coward and would run as soon as he realized that the fight was fair.

He shouted, *"Jackie!"*

No one answered.

Was she dead?

The thought sent bark and bite into Teffinger's brain.

"Jackie!"

The silence fell back into position.

Then he realized how stupid he was. With luck she was hiding. The last thing he wanted to do was bring her out of safety. The second guy must be down by Thumper, looking for her. So far no gunshots had come from that area.

He stood up and slowly eased away from the bottom of the hill, farther out into the road, hoping to get a visual on the man above.

A shot erupted, exploding the dirt mere feet away.

He dived back.

The closest cover in the direction of Jackie was a long ways off, forty steps or more. He'd never make it that far, even if he fired up the whole time.

He was stuck unless he decided to just get stupid and go for it.

He stayed put.

He wasn't any use to Jackie dead.

The seconds ticked off.

The silence reigned.

Then that silence was broken, horribly broken, by two shots that came from back by Thumper.

"Jackie!"

Teffinger's instinct was to get to her. Before he could suppress it, he was on his feet and in the open.

Bam!

Bam!

Bam!

He dived back to cover.

"Jackie!"

19

Teffinger fought to keep his brain from getting jammed into paralysis by emotions. Jackie could be dead or captured. That was a very real possibility. If she were dead, he'd make sure neither man made it out of here alive. The one thing he had going for him was that the Mercedes was sitting on two flats. Thumper was the only way out and even then the Mercedes would have to get pushed out of the way first.

Escape wouldn't be easy, not for anyone.

They were all locked together in a mutual stranglehold, like two pythons trying to squeeze each other to death.

A minute ticked off, then another.

He kept an eye on the road, half expecting Jackie to get pulled around the corner with a gun to her head. At that point they'd call for Teffinger to lay his weapon down, that or watch Jackie's brains get splattered.

What then?

He didn't know.

What he did know is that he needed to do something now, before it got to that point.

He took a deep breath and checked the clip to find only

five bullets left. He couldn't waste a one. Any shot he took needed to be a kill shot. He had no room for brush-back fire or fear shots.

He prepared himself, fully realizing that what he was about to do could very well be his last living act.

Then so be it.

His life had come to this and this was enough.

He wiped the sweat off his brow, got his bearings and busted up the road at sprinter speed.

The gunfire came almost immediately.

He didn't look up.

The first shots missed, then one landed, not directly on his flesh but on the Sig as it swung wildly in his grip, knocking it forcefully out of his hand and several feet to the side. There was no time to get it, not even close. He kept going at full sprint with still thirty steps to go until safety.

He'd never make it.

He was less than a second from being killed.

A boulder appeared on his right, not big, but enough to dive for and at least have partial cover.

Yes or no?

No!

He'd never be able to get back into a sprinting position. He'd be worse off than before.

Keep going!

Keep going!

Keep going!

He kept his knees high and his arms swinging, fully exposed and still twenty steps from safety.

Then a shot rang out and he went down.

His face bounced off a rock with a horrible explosion of

pain.

Then everything turned black.

20

At some point later, which could have been two minutes or two hours, a violent throbbing inside Teffinger's skull pulled him into consciousness. To his shock, next to him, laying face-up in the sun-sizzling dirt and rocks, was the limp body of the gunman from the hill, dead. Two black birds pecked flesh off his face. When Teffinger moved, they hesitated for a moment in defiance before flapping off. The guy's face was half gone, first shot, at least once, and then eaten.

Teffinger muscled into a standing position with a body that screamed but nevertheless functioned.

He remembered the gunshot from above.

He remembered a horrific pain in his ankle that took him to the ground.

He remembered his head slamming into something hard.

He remembered struggling to stay conscious and failing.

He pulled down his sock and checked his ankle. It was a bruised mess and swollen to twice its size but it wasn't shot. Maybe the bullet kicked a rock into it. He didn't know and didn't care. It was already history.

"Jackie!"

No one answered.

"Jackie!"

He headed in her direction. Around the bend, Thumper was still in position, untouched, with the dead bird still on the hood. He went past it and yelled, "Jackie!"

No response came.

He headed farther up the road, past where they'd retrieved the Sig, and spotted a man's body a hundred yards away, laying face up in the sun without motion.

He approached with caution.

"Jackie!"

No one answered.

The man's eyes were open, staring at the sky, waterless and lifeless. His body didn't show any visible trauma, except for his hands, which were covered in blood. It wasn't clear if they'd been injured or just handled something bloody. The man's head hung at an unnatural angle. He had no gun in hand nor was one in the immediate vicinity.

The sight brought a smile to Teffinger's lips.

If both gunmen were dead, Jackie might very well be alive.

"Jackie!"

Silence.

He searched the area.

She wasn't there.

He made his way back to Thumper and thankfully found the keys in the ignition. He fired the beast up and slowly maneuvered it up the road. The dead bird hung tight on the hood longer than it should have before vibrating over to the edge and dropping off.

Around the bend, near the dead face, Jackie came into

sight, walking painfully up the road towards him. Her dress was almost non-existent, her legs were bloody and her arms were cuffed behind her back. Her face was a dirty, sweaty mess and looked like it belonged to someone who had been in the wild for a week.

She focused as if to be sure it was really Teffinger and then collapsed.

21

Teffinger got Jackie up and led her into the shade, then helped her gently to the ground, retrieved the water jug from the back of Thumper and wiped the sweat and dirt and horror off her face and neck and ears. A bloody lip and a punched eye and multiple scrapes came into better focus. Down below, her legs were bloody from deep scratches, almost as if a crazed tiger had gotten a hold of her.

She pulled at the cuffs behind her back.

"Nick, I'm going crazy with these," she said.

He checked to see if he could possibly slide them off. He couldn't, not even close. Her wrists were raw and bloody with fight where they met the metal.

"Wait here."

He got up.

"I already checked for the keys," she said. "I checked both guys and the car. They don't exist. Shoot them off."

Teffinger shook his head.

"Too dangerous. Wait here."

She staggered up.

"I'm coming with you."

Heading up the road, she told him what happened. She'd taken a hiding place but it wasn't a very good one, mostly because there were no good ones.

The guy came for her.

He found her pretty quickly.

She tried to fight him but it was no use. The guy punched her in the face a number of times, slammed her to the ground and cuffed her hands behind her back.

"He was marching me up the road and I dropped to the ground," she said. "When he bent down to yank me up, I kicked him in the face and got him off balance. He fell down and I wrapped my legs around his head and then worked them up like a python, until his face was right in my crotch. I squeezed him in there until he stopped breathing. He tried to shoot me twice but missed. It took a long time to kill him, Nick. It's not like in the movies, ten seconds and it's over. It was more like five minutes. All the time, I could hear gunfire down the road and kept picturing you getting killed."

He could feel the man's fingernails clawing desperately into Jackie's flesh in a frantic effort to break loose.

"I checked the guy's pockets for the keys but couldn't find them, then grabbed the gun and came up the road. You were lying there in the dirt face down and not moving. The other guy was bent over you, checking—I assumed he'd shot you and was making sure you were dead. Then he stood up and pointed the gun at your head, execution style. He didn't see me as I came up. I was almost right on him. I twisted my hands around as far as I could to the side and fired. I don't know how, but I hit him—I think it was in the leg. He went down. I ran over as fast as I could and got to him before he could get to his gun, which had fallen to the side. Then I shot him—the bullet landed in his face, although that's not what I was aiming at, I was just trying to get him anywhere. He fell on his back and didn't move. He looked dead but I put two more in his head, just to be sure. That's it. I checked you and found you were still alive but you were too heavy to pull over into the shade. I checked the guy and didn't find the keys. I figured the Mercedes must be around here some-where and the keys to the cuffs might be in it. I found the car, and the keys were in the ignition but no small one, to the cuffs. Then I headed back to see how you were."

They came to the man with the missing face.

The black birds were back, working feverishly at his flesh, and didn't fly off until the last second.

Jackie was right; she'd got the guy in the leg, which Teffinger hadn't noticed before.

He checked the man's pockets.

There were no keys but he found a wallet, which he stuffed in his pocket without opening it.

He'd look at it later.

They made their way to the second man, the one Jackie suffocated to death.

He also had a wallet, which Teffinger grabbed.

There were no keys in the man's pockets.

There was a small key, however, in the wallet.

It fit the cuffs.

Jackie was free and the look on her face proved it.

She brought her arms forward slowly and rotated her shoulders, loosening up. Then she grabbed Teffinger's hand and said, "Let's get the fuck out of here."

22

Let's get the fuck out of here.

"That's the worst thing we can do," Teffinger said. "We should call the police."

Jackie stepped back.

"Are you crazy?"

"It was self-defense," Teffinger said. "You won't get in any trouble."

The woman shook her head.

"You don't get it, do you? I'm already in trouble. I can't have any cops in my life, period. I got to get to L.A."

"If we run it will catch up to us," he said. "That guy's got a truckload of your DNA under his fingernails. Our blood's in the dirt, both yours and mine. Our prints are everywhere, on the bodies, the gun, the car, who knows where else. I've pissed in the rocks, twice. We couldn't clean this scene in a hundred years. We were here and we can't erase it."

"I don't care about any of that. I just want to get out of here."

"Running will make it worse."

Jackie hardened her face.

"I just saved your ass. Do you appreciate that or not?"

"I do, but—"

"But? There are no buts. I just killed a man for you. Now it's time for you to do something for me. We need to get out of here."

"Trust me, we will," Teffinger said. "If we leave, it will follow us forever. All we need to do is make a report and let the cops do their thing. They'll eventually close the case and we won't have to ever look over our shoulders."

Jackie stomped up the road.

Then she stopped and turned.

"No cops in my life. I already told you that more than once."

Teffinger followed ten steps behind, all the way to Thumper, where the woman got in the vehicle and slammed the door.

"You coming or staying?"

He said nothing.

The woman twisted the key as fast and hard as she could. Thumper sprang to life. She stomped on the accelerator with every muscle in her leg and popped the clutch. The vehicle responded with a violent lunge.

Rocks flew.

Dirt flew.

Teffinger didn't move.

He closed his eyes and let it hit him.

23

Then Teffinger ran, he ran with everything he had, as if his life depended on what happened in the next two minutes—because it did. Jackie was trying to push the Mercedes out of the way with Thumper's front end when Teffinger caught up and got his head in the window.

"Okay, you win," he said.

"Don't do me any favors."

"Look, you're right, you saved my ass. But there's more to it, the part you didn't say."

"Which is what?"

"Not only could I be dead, but you could too. I mean, with your hands cuffed behind your back, you were lucky to get a bullet within ten feet of the guy, much less hit him. If you'd missed, it would have been over that second for both of us, not just me. You only had one chance and it was a long shot but you took it instead of just heading in the other direction until everything was safe. So, you're right. I don't have the right to stand here and be a boy scout and do everything by the book. I don't have the right to be clean while you're dirty."

The woman studied him.

Her face softened.

"I have a plan," Teffinger said. "We'll clean up here and then take the bodies someplace else and bury them."

Jackie shook her head and said, "Look, I don't need to move bodies and all that crap. All I want to do is get out of here and not deal with the cops. I just want to make it to L.A."

Teffinger wiped his brow with the back of his hand.

"It's hot."

"Yeah."

"So that's it? We just leave?"

She nodded and said, "That way you stay clean."

"I don't care about staying clean."

She smiled.

"You're starting to like me," she said.

He shrugged.

"If I am, it's only because I'm alive to do it. So it's your fault."

Teffinger took the wheel and pushed the Mercedes out of the way. Checking the glove box, they found that the vehicle was a rental. They left all the registration papers intact and checked the trunk where they found the wooden box with the skull, which went back into the bed of Thumper. They also found two suitcases in the trunk, packed with clothes and the usual suspects, except for boxes of bullets and one other surprise; an envelope in a secret compartment containing lots of cash, maybe fifty thousand or more.

"We'll leave it," he said.

"Why?"

"I don't want any motive for what happened here except self-defense."

Jackie grabbed the envelope.

"They owe us at least this for what they put us through." She surveyed the terrain and added, "If you're serious about your plan, it might be best, because I'm not going to leave the money here. At least let's clean up."

Over the next hour they erased their presence from the area to the extent feasible—they kicked dirt and rocks over all the areas where their blood or sweat or urine had spilled, they took the cuffs—contaminated with Jackie's blood—with them to dispose of someplace else, they wiped the Mercedes to exhaustion, they made sure they had the Sig, and, as for the guy Jackie smothered, they wiped down his face and neck and hands and underneath his fingernails as best they could, even though in the end it probably wouldn't be good enough, and then covered all the clean area with fresh dirt and smudges.

When it was over Teffinger focused to think if there was anything left to do, couldn't come up with anything, and said, "All the stuff we just erased, it's the stuff that tells the story the way it happened. We basically erased the whole story of how it was self-defense. Damn, that sun's driving me crazy. I can hardly think."

"Forget thinking. Let's just get out of here."

He paced.

Then he shook his head.

"Here's the problem. We can't be halfway pregnant. If we're going to cover up, then we need to do it right. We need to bury the bodies." He got a distant look, then focused and added, "I don't think we have a choice."

"Where? Here?"

He shook his head.

"We can't move the Mercedes, not with two flats, so it needs to be somewhere else."

They got the bodies in the bed of Thumper, covered them in dirt, laid the spare tire and the suitcases on top, and got the hell out of there.

The freeway was largely empty when they came to it, with the exception of an 18-wheeler bearing down at a high speed on the opposite side. The driver threw them a glance but it was quick and non-curious.

"I don't like the bodies back there," Jackie said.

"I can bring them up here if you want."

She punched his arm.

The dirt was blowing around so much that some of it was even sneaking through the shot-out back window.

"I don't know how long we can go before our friends come into view," she said.

Teffinger checked the gas gauge.

It was low.

24

Teffinger focused on the drive, not letting the wobbly front end get into a swerve or do anything else that would draw the attention of a trooper, all the while telling himself that even if they got caught, his downside was limited to losing his job and spending a few years in jail. That was better than being dead, which was exactly where he'd be if it hadn't been for Jackie. Actually, to a point, he was even charged. He owed her and he was paying his debt. He wasn't wimping out on her. He was stepping up, not to mention that if he loved her—and he was pretty sure he did—this was the way to her, by stepping up. They were on a journey, a journey seriously off course to be sure, but a journey that would define whether they belonged together. There were worse places in the universe to be than right here on Thumper's raggedy old bench seat.

The terrain was increasingly desolate.

The traffic was minimal.

The logistics wouldn't get any better.

"Keep your eyes peeled for a place to pull off," he said.

"I already am."

Ten minutes later she pointed and said, "There."

Teffinger slowed down, looked for traffic and saw none. Then he got out, locked the front hubs into four-wheel-drive, and maneuvered off-road into an untouched terrain filled with boulders and uneven plateaus and desert brush. It didn't take long to get out of sight from the road. To their surprise, they came to a steep ravine, forty yards across and an equal distance to the bottom, almost straight down.

Jackie said, "Let's just dump them in."

"And not bury them?"

"I don't think we need to. Do you?"

He considered it.

"Let's go ahead and dump them and then see how it looks."

It was a struggle—getting the spare wheel off the bodies, pulling them out of the truck, dragging them to the edge and then pushing them over and in, where they ricocheted off the unforgiving rock walls on the way down and landed at the bottom with a dead bounce.

Looking at the result, Teffinger soured his face.

"Anyone looking in is going to see them."

"No one's ever going to look in."

He paced and then said, "You never know about a plane or something. We've come this far, let's do it right."

Jackie shook her head.

"This is plenty good. Let the coyotes strip 'em clean."

"I'm not sure coyotes can get down there."

"Birds, then, whatever. Let's just go."

"I'd feel better if they were at least covered with rocks."

"Nick, I'm telling you, this is good enough. Let's just get the hell out of here before someone comes."

He shook his head.

"Wait here. I'm going to see if I can find a way down."

"Nick, let's just go."

"This won't take long; fifteen minutes—"

A hundred steps along the rim, he spotted what could be a viable descent.

His ankle was a mess.

He wasn't sure how much angled pressure he could put on it.

Should he try it or not?

If he didn't, he'd spend the next two years wishing he had.

He took a deep breath, looked quickly for a better option, saw none, and headed down. It was steeper and slipperier than it looked. Halfway down it got even worse and he had to wonder if he could get back up.

Suddenly his ankle slipped out.

He caught himself for a just a second and almost recovered his balance before catapulting sideways into a freefall.

25

Teffinger hit two ledges on the way down, leaving blood and flesh on both but not getting killed by either, or by the final crash into the rocky floor of the ravine for that matter. He didn't hit his head and he didn't break his back and he didn't ugly-up his face. In fact, he got to his feet in pretty good shape, then made his way to the bodies and covered them with rocks, which took over an hour. He found a better way up and made his way to Thumper where an angry but relieved Jackie was waiting for him.

"Kiss me," she said.

He did.

Then he got behind the wheel and they were gone.

There was no traffic in either direction when they got back to the highway.

"I counted the suitcase money," Jackie said.

Teffinger looked over.

"And?"

"Sixty-two thousand, four hundred."

The miles clicked off, every frame picture-perfect, every force of wind through the windows another breath of life, every hum of the tires another symphony. In the distance, a good twenty miles away, a dark thunderhead crept cat-like over a mesa.

Thumper's front end wobbled.

Jackie fell asleep.

Teffinger's thoughts drifted. No one got an enemy like Jackie's without a whole lot of lead-up. She had to have a good idea who was after her. Boudiette fit the bill. Still, Teffinger couldn't shake the feeling that there was a truckload of secrets Jackie wasn't telling him. If that was so then he hadn't gotten through to her yet. She liked him, that was obvious, but he couldn't tell if it would overcome what she planned to do when she got to L.A. She might leave him there. He'd better be prepared for it.

On the other hand, maybe she wasn't the target.

Maybe he was.

He pulled Thumper to a stop on the shoulder and walked a hundred steps into the raw Utah landscape with the cuffs in hand. They'd been wiped clean, but you could never do it a hundred percent. Jackie's blood was still there, not visible to the naked eye, or even the clothed eye for that matter, but big as a billboard to even elementary forensics.

He dropped them behind a rabbit brush, kicked dirt until they were buried, then set a twenty-pound rock on top.

"Rust in peace."

As he headed back to Thumper, Jackie was awake, at first frantic at being stopped and alone, then spotting him walking towards the vehicle.

She ran to him halfway, put him in a hug and said, "Don't be mad at what I'm going to say."

"Huh?"

"I left my cell phone back at the bodies."

"What do you mean?"

"The ravine, the bodies—when you were down there putting rocks on the them, I counted the money. I did that sitting on the ground in the shade, leaning against Thumper's wheel. I had my cell phone next to me on a rock. I forgot to grab it when I got up. It's still there."

Teffinger looked for an excuse to not go back.

They'd already gone miles, many miles.

They'd gotten in there once without being spotted. They might not be so lucky a second time.

Still, the stupid thing was worse than fingerprints.

It would sit there forever, rotting in the sun and the rain, to be sure, but never blowing away.

It had numbers.

Those numbers were linked to Jackie.

If anyone ever spotted the phone, and the bodies, Jackie would immediately be the prime suspect. That would lead to Teffinger as well.

"I know this is a stupid question," he said, "but is the phone registered to you?"

"Yes, I mean, sort of. It's registered to Jackie Jones, but that's not my real name. It's an alias I use."

"What's your real name?"

"It's something different."

"You're not going to tell me?"

"Maybe later but right now I'm freaking out," she said. "The phone can be traced to my alias and my alias can probably be traced to me, if someone digs deep enough. Chances are 99.9 percent that no one is ever going to come across it, and even if they do, they probably won't spot the bodies. But, still, my luck's never that good."

Teffinger exhaled.

"Okay, we'll go back."

"Nick, I'm so sorry. I'm the stupidest person on the face of the earth."

"It's okay. Don't worry about it."

She hugged him.

"Kiss me," she said.

He did, and when he did, he felt a little something he hadn't before.

He was a little closer to her.

She'd let him in just a little more.

Green River was ten miles up the road. The bodies were a hundred miles back. Teffinger checked the fuel gauge, yet again, to find the needle even farther below the E and said, "This is going be close."

He was right.

It was close, but not quite close enough. Two miles short of where they needed to be in Green River, Thumper took its last breath and that was the way the world ended, not with a bang but a whimper. They coasted to the shoulder, hoofed up the road under an unrelenting sun to the first gas station, then back to Thumper, drenched, with a gallon of gas in a discarded milk jug that Teffinger cleaned and wiped dry in the men's room. He poured a little in the carburetor, the rest in the tank and pumped the accelerator as he cranked the key. Thumper choked stubbornly as if drowning and then suddenly leaped to life.

Then it was back to the station for a full tank plus a quart and a half of oil, where Teffinger asked the pimply kid behind the counter, "Is there a place to buy a cell phone in this town?"

"Are you kidding?"

"That's a no?"

The kid nodded.

"It's a big no. Grand Junction, they have them there, or Vegas if you're heading that way. The only thing for sale around here is dead ends. If you want a dead end, we're having a special today—two for the price of one."

Teffinger smiled.

"It sounds like you've been here awhile."

The kid rolled his eyes.

"Mary Lou Wilson," he said. "That's the only good thing in this whole stinking place."

"She's your girl?"

"I'm working on it."

"Not there yet, huh?"

"No." The kid brightened and added, "I've made it to second base though."

"There's nothing wrong with second base," Teffinger said. "That's how I won almost all my games until I was twenty-one, all with singles and doubles." He paid for the gas, handed the kid an extra fifty and added, "Take Mary Lou out for an ice cream. The road to third base is paved with ice cream."

"How about home plate?"

Teffinger frowned.

"That, I'm afraid, takes a lot more than dairy products."

Outside from a payphone, he called 99, real name Samuel Ripper, a private investigator who knew how to not get drunk and blab secrets all over town. The man wasn't cheap but as far as trust and integrity went, he was at the top of the bell curve.

"I have a super-sensitive matter," Teffinger said.

"Why am I not surprised?"

"This has to stay absolutely confidential."

"So no Twitter?"

"No. And no billboards either. How's the cat?"

"Geraldine? She still hates me," 99 said. "Five years I've had that stupid thing and she still hasn't let me pet her once. Get this, though. She loves my new secretary, Gail. I mean absolutely loves her—she curled up in her lap the first time they met. But me? If I get within five feet of her she goes straight into kamikaze mode."

"So why don't you just get rid of her?"

"Do you want her?"

"No."

"There's your answer."

26

It would be a hundred miles at least, back to the bodies, and then they had to figure out where they originally pulled off, if they even could, all under a scorching demon sky. Teffinger could use a long cold shower followed by a long cold beer or two or three followed by a long cold bedroom and a long cold Jackie.

File miles into the drive he said, "I made an executive decision."

She looked over, braced.

"How so?"

"I hired a private investigator in Denver to try to figure out who our two dead friends are."

She tapped her fingers on the clutch.

"What did you tell this investigator, exactly?"

"Not much," Teffinger said. "Just the information from the guys' driver's licenses—their names and addresses—and that I wanted whatever background information he could get on them. That's it. I didn't tell him why I wanted the information."

"Did you tell him they're dead?"

"No."

Jackie looked out the window.

When she turned back, her face was hard.

"You shouldn't have done that," she said. "The names of those two guys should never have come out of your lips, not to this investigator or to anyone else, ever."

"He can be trusted."

"No one can be trusted," she said. "What you've done is connect yourself to those names when you didn't have to."

"We need to figure out who they are," Teffinger said. "That's the only way we can figure out who hired them."

"I already know who hired them—Boudiette."

He exhaled and added, "Maybe yes, maybe no. Either way, they're going to be replaced. More guys just like that will be coming after you. The only way to stop this is to get to the source."

"It's going to come back to haunt us, what you did."

Teffinger patted her leg.

"It's this damned heat," he said. "It turns everything ugly. We're on the right course, trust me."

They ended up going past the turnoff to the bodies. Teffinger realized it when he spotted a butte in the distance that looked like the top of a castle, and remembered that the bodies had been in the back of Thumper when he saw it last.

They did a one-eighty.

Ten miles later Jackie said, "Right there."

Teffinger looked.

The woman was right.

That was the place, no question.

He drove past it for a full mile, then pulled off the road and killed the engine. The plan was to play it safe by keeping Thumper away from the bodies. Teffinger would cut into the terrain on foot and double back out of sight from the highway.

"I'll be back," he said.

Jackie shook her head.

"I'm coming with you."

"No, you need to stay here in case a patrol car comes by. I don't want them towing this thing."

"So what do I say if someone stops?"

"I don't know. Be creative. Just be here with Thumper when I get back."

He got out.

The sun immediately set him on fire.

He grabbed the water jug from the back, drank as much as he could, waited until a car passed and drove out of rearview mirror range, then headed into the devil dirt.

"Don't wear yourself out," Jackie called. "I'm going to dance for you tonight."

He waved.

Then he was out of sight.

The heat grabbed him by the throat and squeezed with a might so terrible that he almost turned back every thirty seconds. The rocks under his feet were so hot that they radiated up with the force of hell. His legs were lead, his pace was a crawl and he wandered off course a lot more than the law allowed. Finally he came to where he wanted to be.

Jackie's phone was there, sitting nonchalantly on a rock.

He powered it up, got a low battery warning, pulled up the contact information for the dead lawyer, Grayson Everly, and wrote down the three phone numbers, which he hadn't had time to do before. As soon as he got the last digit inked on paper the screen went black. He powered it back on and got nothing but an empty stare.

A noise came from down below in the ravine.

He made his way to the edge and looked down to find two mountain lions feeding on the bodies. They had pawed off enough rocks to get their jaws to the flesh.

One looked up with a bloodstained face.

Its eyes met Teffinger's.

He couldn't look away.

It was too surreal.

Then the other one looked up.

He felt the animals' primitive force but wasn't scared. They were down there; he was up here. He expected them to break the stare and return to the flesh. That didn't happen. Instead, one of them growled, paced, and then broke into a sprint along the bottom of the ravine. The other one watched for a second and then followed.

They were heading for a way up.

They were coming for live meat.

27

Teffinger tried to break into a run but the heat had him in a stranglehold and hardly let him move. A frantic jog was all he could manage, and even that didn't last long, reducing itself to something even less. Every few steps he twisted around to see if they were behind him. So far they weren't, but once they had their prey in sight and broke into a full sprint the gap would close fast. They'd knock him to the ground and clamp his throat in their jaws and claw him to death as he fought for air; that's how they'd take him. He had nothing to fight with, *nothing*, not even a stick.

He went straight for the road.

Maybe he'd make it.

If he could get to it, there might be traffic.

It might be enough to scare them off.

How far was it, another half mile?

He ran with everything he had, not caring that he wasn't saving any reserve for a fight because it wouldn't matter. Getting away, that was his only chance.

His lungs burned.

Every muscle in his body screamed with pain.

He was killing himself.

He blocked it out as much as he could.

He couldn't give in to it.

He twisted for a glance behind, fully expecting to see nothing like the last twenty times, but this time realized his worst fears. A hundred yards back, one of the lions was closing in at a fast trot and now picking up speed as it suddenly had Teffinger in sight.

The road was at least a quarter mile away, probably more.

Teffinger stopped and frantically searched for a weapon, spotting nothing except a rock, which he grabbed while he had the chance.

It wasn't big.

It wasn't even baseball-size.

The lion was charging at full speed now.

Its eyes were focused unwaveringly on Teffinger's face and throat.

It charged, closer and closer and closer, getting into a rhythm and gauging the final jumping distance with instincts that went back a million years.

Then it leaped.

Its front legs stretched out.

Its claws extended.

Its mouth opened for the bite.

Its eyes filled with purpose.

Teffinger hurled the rock with every ounce of strength in his body, hoping to land a blow to the beast's forehead, if not strong enough to kill it or knock it out, maybe enough to stagger it.

The rock connected but not at the forehead.

It landed lower, at the animal's mouth, and smashed into its fangs.

It didn't matter.

The animal's forward momentum hit with the force of a telephone pole swinging into Teffinger's chest. The air flew out of his lungs and his body catapulted backwards with the weight of the animal landing on him.

Claws immediately swung and slashed into his leg.

He brought his arms to his neck to shield the lion's mouth from his throat.

The bite didn't come.

Instead the animal convulsed, violently, as if suddenly fighting an invisible demon.

There was something wrong with its breathing.

It was as if it couldn't get air.

Teffinger twisted out from under it and pushed back, away from the claws and fangs as the animal got more desperate in its choking and frenzy, and then finally slumped flat to death.

28

Every molecule of Teffinger's being burned with exhaustion and fatigue and pain. Right here, right now, all he wanted to do was get his face in the shade of a boulder or bush and let his body collapse; that his chest and legs would be in the sun didn't matter. Screw the sun. Screw the heat. Screw everything. He didn't care. He needed to close his eyes and let the darkness sweep him away.

That's what he wanted and all he wanted.

But he got to his feet because he didn't know where the second lion was. Maybe it had turned around, long back—maybe the opposite.

He scanned the horizon and saw nothing.

Five or six large black birds circled above, already sensing the death meal below. Could they actually peck their way through the lion's fur? Probably, otherwise they wouldn't have an interest—unless of course they were there for Teffinger.

He took one last look at the dead lion.

Flies were already on it.

What the hell were they doing out here?

His mind began to wander. It was so stupid that flies were

called flies. Of all the majestic things that flew, from eagles to bumblebees to flamingos to butterflies, why did grammar waste the word fly on such a little irritating piece of crap?

Christ, Teffinger, focus!

The sun's got your brain—

Focus!

He walked off, no longer towards the road, but parallel to it, where he could come out at Thumper. A hundred yards into it he checked his pocket to be sure Jackie's cell phone was still there; good thing too, because it wasn't.

He went back to the lion.

The phone was nowhere.

It wasn't there.

It must have fallen out while he was running. He retraced his steps back to the ravine, all the while keeping a lookout for the second lion. With every step his chest got a little tighter.

Come on!

Where are you!

He wanted to turn around and be done with it all and hated that he couldn't. He kept going, one step, then another, then another, all the way back to the ravine, all the way back to the very rock that he'd picked the stupid thing up from in the beginning.

It was nowhere.

Against his better judgment, he slowly made his way to the edge of the ravine and looked down. What he saw he couldn't believe. Three mountain lions were feeding on the bodies, which they'd now pulled free of all the rocks to where they could get their fangs in good and easy.

One of them looked up at Teffinger.

Their eyes made contact.

He wanted to pull away but couldn't.

It was too surreal.

Then the other two looked up.

29

The problem with Teffinger retracing his steps was that he didn't know exactly where his steps had been. From the ravine he headed back in the direction of the dead lion, which was quite a ways, doing as broad a visual sweep of the ground as the terrain allowed, and all the while keeping a lookout over his shoulder. He had a rock in each hand but knew that he'd never in a million years duplicate what happened before.

The effort was for nothing.

He was all the way back to the dead lion with still no sign of the cell phone.

Come on!

Where are you!

He searched every inch of ground around the lion, extending out a radius of at least fifty feet, well beyond where the phone could have landed, hoping that's where it jumped out of his pocket.

It wasn't anywhere.

He wiped sweat off his forehead with the back of his hand. His throat was sandpaper. His eyes were dry and itchy. The sun was killing him. Not a wisp of wind moved. The air was as quiet as death. The only sound came from the buzzing of flies on the carcass, dozens of them now, the filthy things.

He had a crazy thought, a thought that made him grab the lion's front leg with both hands and drag the carcass until the ground under it showed. No phone came into view where the body had been.

Desperate, he twisted the body over.

The phone appeared, half wedged under the animal's stomach.

Got you, you little bitch.

The screen was shattered but that didn't matter. What mattered was that it was no longer a road sign at a murder scene that pointed to Jackie. He stuck it in his pocket and made sure it was wedged in there nice and tight. It felt good. In fact, everything felt good. It was as if his lungs had more air and his muscles had more power and his brain was more focused.

At Thumper, something bad happened.

Jackie wasn't there.

The keys were in the ignition but she wasn't there.

Jackie!

No one answered.

Jackie!

Jackie!

Jackie!

No sound came, not even the annoying buzzing of a fly.

He searched the nearby brush to see if she was taking a leak. Maybe she went down from a rattlesnake bite or heat exhaustion.

She wasn't anywhere.

She was gone.

Suddenly a vehicle approached from behind.

The top was flat, either from a roof rack or a light bar. As it got closer, it showed itself as a highway patrol vehicle. It pulled up behind Thumper and the lights came on.

A man stepped out.

He was big.

He was ugly.

He didn't look like he enjoyed life very much.

He looked like he was pissed at Teffinger for making him get out of the air conditioning.

30

*Y*ou got a car problem?

That was the question that dripped out of Mr. Ugly's mouth. Teffinger first thought about lying, saying *yes*, but instantly realized that would only encourage the guy to hang around and help, maybe even call for a tow.

"No," he said. "I was getting a little sleepy and pulled over to close my eyes for a few minutes."

The man eyed him.

Teffinger could feel the guy falling into his pattern, getting ready to ask for a license and registration, if he didn't get deflected.

"Damn hot," Teffinger said.

"Yeah. It'll kill you if you're not careful. You got air conditioning in that thing?"

Teffinger looked at Thumper with disgust, shook his head and said, "I don't think they even had it back then."

"They did, but they didn't waste a lot of it on trucks. What happened to your back window?"

"Broke."

"I see that. How?"

"A rock. I'm guessing kids—"

The man looked doubtful, studied the terrain, turned and said, "There's billions of rattlers out there. If you take a leak, do it by your truck. Don't wander out there unless you're super careful."

"I won't."

"I've seen you around someplace before."

Bam!

The words landed like a two-by-four.

Teffinger wrinkled his face, as if it had never been on the cover of GQ or any other piece of paper in the universe, and said, "Well, we all have a twin we never meet."

"No, I've seen you before. What's your name?"

Teffinger's chest tightened.

"Nick."

"Nick, Nick . . . well that doesn't ring any bells, but I know I've seen you someplace. It'll come to me." He dug, came up empty, refocused and said, "Remember what I said about those rattlers. The coroner doesn't really like coming out here. He's fat and doesn't like to move much."

"I get it."

"He heats up like a small planet."

Teffinger pictured it.

Then the man was gone.

At Thumper, Jackie's purse wasn't on the seat where it had last been, but her suitcase was still in the truck's bed. Teffinger checked it to see if the envelope of the dead guys' money was still there, the $62,400.

It wasn't.

Jackie was gone.

All the money was gone.

She'd abandoned him.

Maybe some edgy young stud on a Harley stopped to see if she needed help, and everything changed, just like that.

Who knows?

Who cares?

He studied the horizon.

Then he fired up the engine, did a one-eighty, and headed east, back to Denver.

The ride was over.

31

Twenty miles down the road, Teffinger had a crazy thought and twisted around to see if the box with the skull was still in the back of the truck.

It was, wedged against the tire.

He pulled to the side, left the engine running and opened it to see if the skull was still inside.

It was.

The sight made him smile ever so slightly.

Jackie would have taken it if she'd been able to.

Maybe she didn't find a better offer after all.

Maybe something happened.

He did another one-eighty and headed west.

The more he thought about it, the more he convinced himself that something must have happened. Sure, Jackie had pictures of the skull, but they were on her cell phone, which she didn't have—he did. Plus, it was unlikely she would have run off without first knowing her phone was no longer at the scene. Teffinger's heart lightened. Whatever happened, it no longer felt like a punch in the gut.

It felt more like trouble.

He sped up to fifty-five but the front end wobbled with so

much protest that he had to cut back. A red 18-wheeler came up from behind and shot by at eighty with stripper mud flaps doing nothing to stop a rock from kicking up into Thumper's front end.

A mile clicked off, then another and another.

Then something strange happened.

A mile or so up ahead, a red 18-wheeler—no doubt the one with the stripper flaps—was pulling from the shoulder back onto the highway from the place where Thumper had been parked when Jackie disappeared.

Had the guy spotted something and stopped to get it. Jackie's purse, maybe?

Teffinger sped up.

The front end got violent, so violent that the 18-wheeler got up to speed before Teffinger could catch it. He pulled over where the truck had been and got out.

Jackie!

No one answered.

He scouted around and spotted nothing but nature. The ground had no wet spots. The trucker hadn't stopped to take a piss. That didn't mean anything though. Maybe the guy pulled over to check a tire, or secure a chain, or whatever. Maybe it was nothing more than a coincidence that it happened here, exactly where Thumper had been. Deep down, though, Teffinger didn't want it to be a coincidence. He wanted it to have something to do with Jackie.

He got back in Thumper and drove.

The 18-wheeler was a mere dot in the distance at this point.

Within ten minutes it was gone altogether.

The miles passed.

Then something white appeared in the dirt at the side of the road, something strange enough out here in the middle of nowhere for Teffinger to give it a solid look as he sped past.

What the hell?

He slammed on the brakes, backed up at full speed and squealed to a twisting stop.

The white thing was a dress.

It looked like Jackie's.

There was a bloodstain on the front.

Teffinger tossed it into the cab through the window, scrambled back in and popped the clutch.

32

Teffinger kept Thumper hammered to the verge of rattling apart, knowing full well he could never catch the truck but desperate to keep the gap to a minimum. The miles clicked off and no turnoffs came, not a one. The truck never came into sight, not even when the road crested and the view opened up.

Curves came, winding through an increasingly moon-like topography.

They were good.

They would slow the truck.

Traffic was almost non-existent.

Suddenly a figure appeared in the road up ahead.

Jackie?

Yes, it was actually her, running towards him and then suddenly there, right at the window, as he squealed to a stop.

"Nick!" she screamed.

Horror etched her face.

"What the hell?"

He jumped out and squeezed her tight, feeling trembles from her body. She had her purse in hand but was wearing no clothes, not a stitch. A large cut on her forehead sent blood down her face.

"Jackie . . ."

He got her into a new dress from the suitcase and cleaned her face while she told him what happened.

"I saw you in the rearview mirror. I knew you were coming."

"So you were in the truck?"

"Yes. I turned the wheel."

"What's that mean?"

"It means I grabbed the wheel and crashed us."

Teffinger looked, saw no crashed truck but did see tracks heading off a hundred yards or so where they disappeared into something that could be a drop-off or large arroyo.

"It's over there?"

"Yes."

"What about the driver?"

She exhaled.

"I think he's dead."

"You think or you know?"

"I think . . . he was bloody and he wasn't moving."

Teffinger's eyes fell to the terrain. Jackie must have read his thoughts because she said, "You were gone way too long. I pictured you bitten by a rattlesnake or something, so I headed out see if you were okay. I got seriously disoriented and when I finally made it back, Thumper was gone and you were nowhere around."

"I thought you took off," Teffinger said

"Why?"

He shrugged.

"Because when I got back, you were gone, the money was gone—"

"When I went to look for you, there was no place to lock

the money up and I didn't want to just leave it there in the suitcase," she said. "So I put it in my purse and hid it out a ways behind one of those bush-things so I didn't have to carry it."

He kissed her.

"Stay here."

"Where are you going?"

"To check on the driver."

"No," she said. "He's dead."

"You said you weren't sure—"

"I'm sure enough. He was going to kill me, Nick. If he is alive by some freak of nature, just let him be."

He hesitated.

"Why do you say he was going to kill you?"

"For the money, Nick. For the money."

"Stay here."

"No! If you're going, I'm going."

Jackie filled in more of the blanks as she and Teffinger picked their way into the terrain.

She didn't want to get into the 18-wheeler when it pulled over to her.

The guy looked too freaky with all his tattoos and his fat hairy neck and that big old beer-belly gut hanging out over his fat old crotch.

But Thumper was gone and the guy kept smiling and insisting, and the sun was so damn hot, and she was so damned tired, and she could feel the air conditioning coming out the window, and the radio was playing Achy Breaky Heart, and there was nobody else coming up the road and there hadn't been for a long time.

So she got in, clenched her purse in her lap and sat as

close to the door as she could.

First came small talk—innocent, harmless and even friendly—but within a few miles, the truck was up to 90 and just like that the man's hand was on Jackie's knee and it wouldn't come off.

Then he jerked her dress up and said, "Let's see what we got up here."

She struggled.

Her purse opened.

The envelopes came into view.

He grabbed one.

"What's this?"

"Nothing."

He landed a backhand to her face and tore the envelope open as blood from her nose fell down onto her dress.

"Nothing, huh?"

She opened the door to jump out but he got her by the hair at the last second and yanked her back.

Then he pulled a gun from somewhere to his left, maybe the door panel, and a sick smile came to his face.

"Do that again, please. I don't mind cleaning up the splatter. I really don't. It only takes thirty minutes."

When he found out there was a ton of money, he made her take off her clothes—all of them; the dress, the panties, the bra—and throw them out the window.

Then he got real quiet and he kept checking his rearview mirrors.

"He was trying to figure out where to pull over and kill me," Jackie said. "His puny little cock was sticking up. When I saw a chance to yank the wheel, I did it. I didn't care if the crash killed me. At least he'd be getting a face-full of it too. Fuck him."

The crash scene materialized up ahead. The trailer part of the rig was largely undamaged. The weight of it, though, had pile-driven the cab down a long sloping embankment and directly into a rock wall, smashing the cab horribly. The driver was halfway through the windshield, with his torso immobile on the hood and his legs still inside on the dash.

He looked dead.

Teffinger approached slowly, looking for movement or signs of life, and then nudged the body as he said, "Hey, buddy."

Suddenly the man's eyes opened and looked directly into Teffinger's.

33

The man's eyes coming open in that dead face was so freaky and unexpected and horror-charged that something deep down in Teffinger's caveman genes recoiled him backwards.

"He's alive."

"Yeah, I see."

Teffinger came closer.

The man's eyes blinked but other than that every square inch of his body remained utterly and one hundred percent immobile.

Teffinger poked the man's arm to see if it would spark a reaction.

It didn't.

Jackie grabbed Teffinger's arm, pulled him to the side and said, "Let's get out of here."

"You mean leave him?"

"Yeah, leave him. We don't have a choice," she said.

Teffinger paced.

"Christ—"

"We can't help him," Jackie said. "He's way too fucked up."

Teffinger couldn't deny it.

The guy looked paralyzed.

Still, if they just left him, it might take a long time for him to die.

"Look," he said. "Let's get to the highway, flag down a car and have them call it in."

"No because that will connect us."

"We'll just say we saw the truck veer off."

"Nick, you know that won't work. My prints are in there, my blood is in there—we need to get out of here and I mean now. Every minute that Thumper is sitting up there right where the accident happened is putting us more and more in danger."

He wrinkled his brow.

The words were true.

If they'd been smart, they would have driven Thumper a mile or so up the road before checking on the wreck. Still, the man was alive and was suffering.

Jackie walked over to him.

"Can you move anything?"

The eyes looked at her but nothing on the man's body moved.

"He's paralyzed," she said.

Teffinger nodded.

She turned back to the man and said, "If you can understand what I'm saying, I want you to blink your eyes twice."

The man complied.

"Okay," she said. "I'm going to ask you a question. If the answer is yes, I want you to blink your eyes twice. If the answer is no, I want you to blink your eyes three times. Do you understand?"

The man blinked his eyes twice.

"Good," Jackie said. "That was a yes, right?"

The man blinked twice.

"Okay, hold on."

She surveyed the terrain for a cactus, broke off a three-inch needle and dangled it in front of the man's face. "Now, here's the question and I want you to be totally honest. I can't emphasize how important it is that you answer the question truthfully. If you lie, I'm going to know it, and I'm going to spend the rest of the day sticking this needle in your eyes. If you tell the truth, though—which you'd better—you're going to get some options, and things will be a lot better for you. Do you understand?"

The man blinked twice.

"Good," Jackie said. "Now, here's the question. Were you going to kill me?"

The man's eyes watered.

"Answer!"

He blinked twice.

Jackie said to Teffinger, "Did you see that?"

He nodded.

"Yeah, I saw it."

Back to the man, Jackie dropped the needle to the ground and said, "That was smart to answer truthfully. That brings us to the next step. We're either going to leave here without touching you and let whatever happens naturally happen, for however long it takes. Or, if you want, I can put you out of your misery by bashing your head in with a rock. Do you understand the two choices?"

The man blinked twice.

"Okay," Jackie said. "You understand. Now, if you want us to just walk away, I want you to blink twice. If you want me to smash your head in with a rock, I want you to blink three times."

The man blinked, three times.

"Smart choice," Jackie said.

She hunted the ground until she found a rock the size of a softball. Then she looked the man in the eyes and said, "I got to be honest with you, this is going to be sweet. I'm almost getting an orgasm."

34

Teffinger grabbed the rock just as Jackie was cocking her arm to swing it down into the man's skull.

"Don't."

"Let me go!"

He pried it out of her grip and tossed it to the side. "Look," he said, "if you do it, it will be a homicide—even though he asked for it and even though it'll be a mercy kill, it'll still be a homicide. So far, by jerking the wheel, you've done nothing wrong. That was self-defense all day long. He even admitted he was going to kill you, if it ever comes to that— I'm a witness. But if you bash his head in, then you're dirty; you've committed a homicide. It's not worth it. Once you get the dirt on you, it never comes off."

"I don't care."

"You should," Teffinger said. "Like you said, your blood's in the cab. You're connected to the crash. If you bash his head in, any coroner worth his salt is going to figure out that the rock was the cause of death. There will be rock debris embedded in his skin. We couldn't wipe it out even if we wanted to. Everything will point to the fact that someone bashed his head in. So, who was here to do it? According to the blood in the car—the blood that isn't his—it was you."

"I'll be a million miles away."

Teffinger shook his head.

"You're never a million miles away," he said. "You're a knock-on-the-door away. And it's no different if I bash him in instead of you. It'll come back on you because it's your blood in the cab."

She studied the ground and then brightened.

"What if we suffocate him?"

Teffinger shook his head.

"Dirt is dirt," he said.

"No, let me play it out," Jackie said. "We can put something in his mouth and let him choke on it, a piece of windshield glass or something like that. Since he got paralyzed, he couldn't get it out. It'll be just like he got killed from the crash."

Teffinger pictured it.

It was better than the rock, evidence-wise; but it was still dirt.

"No," he said.

"What then?"

He grabbed her hand, pulled her away from the truck and said, "Come on."

Ten steps away he turned and took one last look.

The man's eyes were wide open, watching them leave.

35

A hundred yards away from the crash Jackie said, "Hold on a minute," turned, and trotted back towards it, her dress bouncing high as it swung from side to side. Teffinger watched, unable to follow thanks to the sun's stranglehold, and at this point no longer caring except to summons one shout, "Don't!"

The woman didn't turn or slow down.

So be it then; if she was hell-bent on getting her orgasm, then go get it. Teffinger had made his case. He was through with it at this point.

Five minutes later the woman returned.

In her right hand was a gun.

In her left hand were two boxes of bullets.

She handed them to Teffinger and said, "Carry these for me, will you?"

The weapon was a 9mm Glock with a full clip, ready to do whatever it was told to do. Teffinger shoved it in his belt and said, "How was our friend?"

"There were a couple of black vultures or something on his back that flew off when they saw me. I'm sure they're back by now."

They kept walking.

When they got within sight of Thumper, Teffinger's chest tightened. There at the truck was the same state trooper who stopped him before. His vehicle was behind with the lights flashing. He was already out, staring in Thumper's window like a snake locked on a mouse.

Jackie—if she suddenly walked out of the desert at Teffinger's side, the trooper would want to know where she'd been before, the first time he stopped at Thumper. The truth—*We got separated dumping two dead bodies in a ravine*—wasn't an option. Even if they had the time to come up with good lies, they would eventually circle back around to the truth. Jackie needed to never be seen anywhere around this part of the universe; that was the only option.

"Here's the plan," he said. "Stay out of sight and make your way down the road. I'll deal with this guy and then pick you up as soon as I can. Stay off the road. Don't swing into sight until I get close. Can you do that?"

"Yes."

He kissed her.

"Try to get as far away as you can, a mile or whatever."

"Okay."

"If you miss me when I go past—or if there's another vehicle on my tail and I don't slow down—just stay out of sight. I'll swing back for you."

"Okay."

He grabbed her elbow and said, "Here's the most important part. Don't get in any trucks, even if they have candy."

She punched him.

"Not funny."

He smiled.

"It will be later."

"If there is a later—"

"There will be."

The woman got a look on her face, a bad look, and said, "Nick, I did something stupid."

"Like what?"

"Like bashing the guy's head in."

"You're kidding me—"

"Unfortunately I'm not."

"I told you not to. I thought we agreed."

"It wasn't my fault."

"What?"

"I looked into his eyes to see if he was still alive. When he was, something snapped. It happened, just like that. I only went back to get the gun. That's the honest truth. I didn't go back to kill him. Everything else just happened before I even knew it was happening. The whole thing was like, I don't know, all of five seconds. I wiped the dirt off his head though, like you said."

"I never said to do that because I never said to bash him."

"Yeah, I know, but you mentioned it, so I did it."

Teffinger exhaled.

"What'd you wipe him with?"

"My dress."

"Show me where, exactly."

"Down here."

It was at the bottom and barely visible, although there was clearly a discolored smudge that could have contained the man's skin or even his blood.

Teffinger tore the section out and put it in Jackie's hand.

"Get down the road like I said. Bury this as deep as you

can and put a rock over it. Don't do it anywhere around here. Get away as far as you can before you do it."

Her eyes watered.

"Nick, everything's caving in."

"Just stay calm. It'll work out. Now go."

She kissed him.

Then she was gone, with the purse in one hand and the Glock in the other.

36

effinger waited until Jackie got a safe distance and then ran into the trooper's view shouting, "Hey! There's been a crash!"

The guy immediately snapped into the moment and said, "Where?"

Teffinger pointed.

"An 18-wheeler. The driver went through the windshield. I think he's dead."

"Where? I don't see anything—"

"There's a drop-off."

"Wait here."

The man made a hurried, no-nonsense radio call from his vehicle and then headed into the terrain as he shouted to Teffinger, "Come on, show me."

Teffinger led the way; a fast walk, that's all they could summons given the god-forsaken inferno all around them. Teffinger shot glances to the left to be sure Jackie was out of sight. To his horror, she was a good distance off but still in visual contact, focused on the direction she was going and oblivious to what was behind her. Teffinger got on the other side of the trooper to keep the man's glance away from Jackie and said, "You got an ambulance coming?"

"Flight for life."

The words hit with the impact of a tire iron.

Jackie would be visible from the sky.

Worse, she might be spotted before she even knew there was anything up there looking down, if the sound was going the other direction. If she got spotted—even once, even for one second—she'd be hunted down. It was too much of a coincidence that she was out here to begin with, much less that she was heading away from the scene of a fatal crash. If she went down, Teffinger would be right behind her—he was already an accessory at this point, more than once if anyone was counting.

The crash appeared in the terrain up ahead.

Teffinger pointed to the obvious and said, "There."

"Yeah, I see."

They slowed when the driver came into view, grotesquely splayed over the hood and as still as death itself. Two large black birds were on his back, defiantly owning him before squawking off.

Teffinger looked for the rock impact.

It was there on the man's forehead.

The man's eyes were open, as before, but no longer blinking and already dried and shriveled from the sun. His body was in the exact position as before. None of his immobile parts had sparked to life. He was actually better off dead if the truth be told.

The trooper felt for a pulse, got nothing, and focused on the birds perched on a rock thirty yards off, waiting.

"So you saw what happened?"

"Sort of," Teffinger said. "I was behind him quite a ways—a half mile or so, maybe—when he suddenly turned to the right. At first I thought there was a turn off or something but then I saw the way everything was bouncing."

"Were there any other cars around him?"

"Not that I saw."

"You weren't by him, right? He wasn't avoiding you?"

Teffinger shook his head.

"I was way behind him, like I said."

"You weren't trying to pass him or anything like that?"

"No, I was way behind him."

"So why'd he veer off?"

"I don't know. Maybe an animal jumped out in front of him."

"Did you see an animal?"

"No, I didn't see anything. All I saw was the truck jerking off the road."

The trooper surveyed the cab to be sure there was no one else to be worried about, and said, "Remember when I said I'd seen you around somewhere?"

"Yeah."

"I remembered where it was," he said. "I was in San Francisco four years ago. You were part of a panel on homicide investigations."

Teffinger nodded.

"That was me."

The man extended his hand and said, "Charles Taggert. Everyone calls me Tag."

"Nick Teffinger."

"Teffinger, yeah, I remember now. It was pretty fascinating, actually. You still doing them?"

"Here and there but not as much."

"I even started thinking about getting into a big city," Tag said. "That didn't last long. I'd miss the heat and the space."

"The space I can understand although I'll be honest, it makes me feel small."

"It's the opposite with me. Buildings make me feel small."

A rumble snuck into the quietness.

Off in the distance, the very far distance, a speck appeared in the sky.

The sound was coming this way, giving good warning, but it was coming from the direction Teffinger didn't want—it would pass directly over Jackie.

"One of the things I remember from your talk is that every fatality is initially treated as a homicide scene, until it's found to be something else."

"Right."

"Maybe you could hang around a little and give me a few pointers—"

"Single vehicle crashes like this," Teffinger said, "they're almost always the driver falling asleep. Look around the cab. I'll bet dollars to donuts you'll find uppers somewhere."

"You said he suddenly veered off, right?"

"Right."

"If he fell asleep he'd leave the road more gradually, don't you think?"

"He could have woken up and panicked. It could have been a heart attack, too—the guy's obviously a candidate—or a mechanical failure, or a suicide, or even a fly."

"A fly?"

"Didn't you ever get a fly in the cabin, or a bee? You start swatting at it and then suddenly, *wham*! You're in trouble.

It's happened to me more than once," Teffinger said. "I can guarantee you that. Don't spread it around though."

The guy pictured it and smiled

"What a way to go—killed by a fly."

"I'm sure it's happened," Teffinger said. "The ironic thing is, the fly probably lives 99 percent of the time."

"That would be downright embarrassing."

Teffinger nodded.

"If your relatives didn't like you, it'd be right there on your tombstone for the rest of your non-life—Killed by a Fly."

"Ouch."

"Major ouch."

The speck in the sky was no longer a speck; it was a helicopter now.

Teffinger wiped his brow with the back of his hand.

"The sun's a vampire."

Be hidden, Jackie.

Be hidden.

Be hidden.

Be hidden.

37

The flight-for-life guys, a man and a woman actually, didn't take long to pronounce the driver dead at the scene. The third person—the pilot—watched quietly as everyone worked, then told Tag, "When we were coming in, I'm pretty sure I saw someone down on the ground."

Tag focused on him.

"Where?"

"Up the ways a mile or so. I think it might have been a woman."

"A woman?"

"Yeah, I think so."

"By herself?"

"I think so. I didn't see anyone else. She was out in the desert, fifty or a hundred yards off the road. It was real strange because there were no cars pulled over to the side or anything like that. It was just her way out there all alone in the desert."

"Maybe a hunter?"

The man shrugged.

"Wasn't wearing orange." He shook his head. "It was just strange."

Teffinger jumped in and said, "Was she waving for help or anything?"

"No."

Tag lost interest.

"Probably a rattlesnake poacher," he said. "That's how they work. Someone drops them off and then swings back in a couple of hours. As far as I'm concerned, they can have every one of those little fuckers. My cousin lost a leg to one when he was only ten; saddest thing I've ever seen."

There are times in life when one moment turns into the next and the next and the next, all in a long straight continuous line, with no place to jump off or change course, no matter how much you want to. For Teffinger, this was one of those times. Tag wanted to write down a quick statement for Teffinger to sign, but first everyone got busy trying to drag the 250-pound body into the cab, only to get the gut hung up on something. Reversing the plan they pulled it onto the hood where it laid quietly for a second and then suddenly slipped off and crashed to the ground.

The man's face smacked against the fender on the way down, snapping his skull back with a blow that would have killed him if he hadn't been dead already. Then that same face smashed straight down at full gravitation force directly into a rock.

The shattering of bone sounded like glass dropping.

The two birds jumped into the air and flapped away like the devil was on them.

It was pure poetry.

"Oops," Tag said.

They rolled the carcass over.

The face, fairly normal before, was now in ruins.

38

Rattlesnake!

That's what Teffinger should have done, he should have shouted rattlesnake! and pointed frantically at a distant cactus or bush—that would have pulled Tag over to shoot the fangs out of the little devil's mouth, it would have given Teffinger time to grab the bills, it would have been all he needed. That's not what he did, though. Instead he didn't do anything, because the heat had his brain.

Tag was at the cab's door, already looking in and spotting the bills.

His face brightened.

"Whoa, look at this."

Teffinger cast his eyes on the bills, ostensibly for the first time, and said, "Looks like the fat man left you a tip."

Tag leaned in the picked the bills up, seven of them, all hundreds.

"Didn't expect this," he said.

Teffinger wiped his brow.

"Hooker money," he said.

"You think?"

"That or drugs. Either way, he doesn't need it anymore."

The man studied Teffinger, as if deciding, and said, "A tip, huh?"

Teffinger nodded.

"I never saw nothing, so don't worry about me."

"We'll split it," Tag said.

Teffinger shook his head.

"You're the one who earned it," he said.

The man peeled off three, handed them to Teffinger and said, "We both earned it."

Teffinger hesitated, then took the bills and shoved them in his wallet and said, "Thanks."

Tag put the other four into his pocket.

It was the most beautiful sight Teffinger had ever seen.

They searched the rest of the cab and found no more bills or anything of interest, other than a small, unlabeled container of yellow pills, which they suspected to be uppers, and a box of 9mm bullets—but no gun.

"Weird, bullets but no gun," Tag said.

They checked the adjacent terrain.

If the weapon had been ejected, they couldn't find it.

Tag's radio crackled and the pilot's voice came through, barely audible above the roaring of the blades. "Hey, about that woman," he said.

Tag scrunched his face and focused on the aircraft a mile or two off, hovering low.

"Is she okay?"

"I don't know. We can't find her. I'm thinking someone might have picked her up."

Tag considered it.

"Do another sweep," he said. "You got gas?"

"Plenty."

"Give it some more time, then. I'm worried she might have gotten bit. I'd hate to think you were right there and then flew off while she was dying. How ironic would that be?"

"We're going lower."

Teffinger's heart raced.

Jackie must have found a good hiding place, but it wouldn't be good from every angle.

Suddenly something happened that he didn't expect.

A hand came out from under the truck and briefly squeezed his ankle before disappearing again just as fast.

He knew that hand.

It belonged to Jackie.

39

Vegas at night was a place like no other. The buzz, the lights, the pretty-pretty people, the over-the-top everything, the never-ending party and the chance that you could end up owning the whole freaking place if everything somehow went batshit crazy. It was all a toxic firestorm for the blood. Teffinger and Jackie pulled into the thick of that craziness an hour after dark, road-beaten to death but alive. They ventually ended up in an air-conditioned contemporary room on the 15th floor of the Cosmopolitan, on the strip side of the building, hovering above Las Vegas Boulevard with a view that looked like they were coming in for a landing.

They showered the day off with long, hot, endless soul-soaking water, not getting out until their cuts and scrapes and bruises and pains were flooded and flushed ten times over. Even with that, they both looked liked they'd been in a fight, and not on the winning side. Teffinger had already gotten dirty looks—the woman beater.

They filled their stomachs with room service.

Scrubbed up, in jeans and a black tee and a bounce back in her step, Jackie was perfect; swollen lip, black eye and all.

She was worth every stupid thing that Teffinger had done in the last however-many insane hours he'd know her.

Still, they'd been lucky; things could have gone wrong a hundred different ways and the stark reality of that simple fact, when it bubbled its way to the surface, felt like broken glass inside Teffinger's throat.

He choked it down.

They were safe now.

That's what mattered.

Plus, now they had history together.

If that didn't break Teffinger through into the woman, nothing would.

"At some point, you're going to have to tell me exactly what you did that has you so afraid to get arrested," he said.

She studied him.

"There's only one thing you need to know," she said.

"And what's that?"

"That I'm horny like I've never been in my life."

"Oh?"

She ran a finger down his chest. "I need someone to un-horny me. Do you want to apply for the job?"

"Let me get my resume out."

On the balcony, with the sound of the city weaving up through the air, he did the job, long and slow, and with every molecule of his being. Then total exhaustion took them within seconds, right where they were, and everything turned wonderfully black and peaceful.

DAY THREE

July 9
Friday

40

Friday morning while Jackie was still sleeping, Teffinger made his way down into the guts of the hotel where he found a payphone and called the investigator—99—who had some interesting news.

"Okay, both of your friends were using fake identities. One of them, William Tate, I still don't have a clue who he is. The other one, though, *Nate Brown*—his real name is Sean duGrom; he's an ex-FBI guy."

"Christ."

"That's about all I got on him so far, other than his address."

Teffinger exhaled, weighing how much more information to give the man.

"Okay, he said. "Keep what I'm about to tell you confidential. Don't write it down, I don't want any records anywhere. DuGrom is a hit-man. His mark was either me or a Chicago woman named Jacqueline Angelica, who also goes by the alias Jackie Jones. See if you can find out who hired him. It might be a French man named Boudiette, but I'm not sure about that one way or the other."

"Is the woman dead?"

"No. Why?"

"You said, *was*," 99 said.

"Huh?"

"You said his mark was a woman named Jacqueline Angelica, past tense. I figured he got her."

Teffinger's chest tightened.

He should have said, is—his mark is a Chicago woman named Jacqueline Angelica.

"Forget the grammar," Teffinger said. "Find out who hired him. Pay a visit to his house. Where's he live?"

"Daytona Beach."

"Florida?"

"Yeah. We're talking about a plane trip—"

"That's fine."

"Not from where I sit. I hate air, you know that."

Teffinger tightened his voice and said, "Yeah, I do. Put a bag of food out for Geraldine before you leave, just in case you crash; no use both of you suffering."

99 chuckled and said, "I'm doubling my price."

"That's fine because I'm only paying half."

Across the way, a woman in her late-20s stepped out of the restroom, fluffing long, thick, pitch-black hair as she walked. Every eye in the place, both male and female, was already on her. She was that kind of woman—the island girl that sailors killed for, the runway model who could care less, the girl next door who inspired every pin-up drawing since the dawn of time.

London Stone?

Yes, it was her.

The sight pulled up a memory so vivid that it was as if Teffinger was right there. It was a Friday night. The club was large and packed and crazy with pounding bass and gyrating bodies and out-of-control hormones. Perfume and pot and sex wove through the air. Pretty-pretty faces and prime bodies decked out in teasing flesh filled every frame. He had three Buds in his gut and a fourth in his hand and was primed for the kill.

Suddenly arms wrapped around him from behind and a body grinded against him, at one with the music.

He didn't turn.

He took a sip from the blue can and let it happen.

That continued for a full song, then another, and then the body pulled away.

Teffinger turned.

No one was there, just the crowd.

That was his first encounter with London Stone.

He shook the vision off, hurried up behind her and tapped her shoulder as he said, "Excuse me Ms., I think you broke a heart back there." She turned and focused, initially confused, then putting him a tight, full-body squeeze before pulling back and gauging him up and down, obviously not too displeased at what she saw, in spite of the mess to his face.

"Nick Fucking Teffinger," she said.

"London Fucking Stone," he said.

"What'd you do? Get on the wrong side of Bad, Bad, Leroy Brown?"

He smiled.

"Something like that. What are you doing in Vegas?"

"Business." She ran a finger down his nose. "Maybe now a little pleasure too."

Teffinger soured his face.

"I'm sort of with a traveling companion," he said.

"A woman?"

He nodded.

London shrugged.

"Bring her along."

"That's a great plan on paper but probably not so much in reality."

The woman put disappointment on her face, licked his ear, and whispered, "Too bad. I saw you on GQ. It got me thinking again." She looked at her watch, wrinkled her nose and added, "At least let's all get together for supper or a glass of wine or something. I'm staying at the Paris, 1420."

"Okay."

"Give me your number," she said.

"I lost my phone but I'll call you later at your room."

"Promise?"

"Promise."

She kissed him.

Then she was gone.

He called Sydney, gave her the three numbers from Jackie's cell phone, and said, "I think these numbers all belong to the dead lawyer in Chicago."

"Grayson Everly?"

"Yeah, that one. Verify it one way or the other and get whatever records you can."

"Should I bring Vine in on it?"

Good question.

He pondered it and said, "Not yet."

Sydney hardened her voice. "Teff, get yourself out of love with this woman. Do it now while you still can."

He considered it.

Then he said, "Too late."

"It's never too late."

"This time it is. Has been, in fact."

Across the way, London was almost out of sight. Two men in sunglasses were in her wake, ten steps back, staring directly at her as they followed. It was probably just a case of male eyes taking in the sights of a perfect female posterior, but there were no smiles or banter. Their clothes were layered and baggy, the kind you'd wear if you wanted to conceal a gun.

He headed in that direction, no doubt working his way into nothing more than a brief waste of time, but with a brisk pace nonetheless.

41

The two men were definitely on London's tail, following her down the strip, across Las Vegas Boulevard and into the Paris, where the woman made her way into the parking garage and disappeared in a red Camry.

The men walked the stairs up a level and left in a black BMW with dark windows and a tinted license plate cover. London had too much of a head start for the guys to follow, unless they had stuck a tracker on her car or knew where she was going.

Okay, so now what?

The men had never closed the gap or made an aggressive move. Still, there'd been people around the whole time and that could be why.

He made his way to the front desk, and after talking to three different people and showing his homicide credentials, got the number they had on file for London Stone and called to tell her how she'd been followed.

At the end she said, "No, I have no idea who they are."

"Come on, London."

"Honest, Nick."

"Are you in some kind of trouble?"

"Christ, Nick. It's possible. You know what I do for a living."

"Actually, I don't."

"Well, I'll catch you up later. Right now I got to go."

The line died.

It died before he could tell her the most important part.

He dialed back and got dumped into voicemail where he left a warning for her to watch out for a black BMW.

He walked down the strip until he found a place to buy a new cell phone. He dialed London from it, got voicemail again, and left a message as to what his new number was.

On the walk back to the Cosmopolitan, he got no calls, but sensed motion directly behind him.

"Hey, pretty boy," someone said.

He turned just in time to see a fist swinging at his face. It landed with a fierce velocity, knocking him wildly off his feet and violently bouncing the side of his head off the concrete.

"You've been warned!"

Back at the room, Jackie was a fury of motion, throwing her things into her suitcase and not caring about Teffinger's bloody head. Her eyes shot devil sparks.

"I Googled you," she said.

"And?"

"Architect my ass. Nick Derringer, architect. That's what you told me."

He flashed back to the bar, when he met her.

He had no recollection of what he told her but could have well said what she said. He'd used that line before.

"You're actually a homicide detective," she said.

He nodded.

"That's true."

She shook her head in disbelief.

"You're working with that detective back in Chicago, aren't you? That guy Vic Vine— That's what this is about. It's all smoke and mirrors so you and your little buddy detective can get up close and personal and figure out if I killed that lawyer."

The words slammed into Teffinger's brain.

How would she know anything about the dead lawyer unless she was the one who killed him?

"You're talking about Grayson Everly," he said.

Her eyes flashed.

"So you know his name," she said. "That proves it." She swung the suitcase up, headed for the door and said, "Have a nice life. Or, better yet, don't."

Then she was gone.

42

The inside of Teffinger's cranium beat with little demon drums, possibly from a concussion. He eased backwards onto the mattress, brought his head lightly to the pillow and closed his eyes. The silence was deafening. Just like that, everything had gone to shit. Everything he'd done over the last few days—all the illegal acts, moving the bodies, the whole trucker incident, lying to troopers—they were all for nothing. It was his own fault. Sure, he'd fallen in love with the woman and that was a lot of the reason he was with her, the majority, actually, but a small part of him, a part he couldn't turn off, was hunting her as well. He couldn't deny it.

Jackie.

Jackie.

Jackie.

Her not being there in the room, her not loving him in that oh-so-easy way of hers, it was too unbearable. It was death by a thousand cuts with a new one slicing into his brain every second the woman wasn't there.

He couldn't take it, not one minute more.

He shot up out of bed.

The room spun.

He shook it off, bounded out the door without closing it, bypassed the elevator and ran down the stairs three at a time, all the way to the parking garage.

Thumper was in motion, almost gone, heading out of the florescent lighting and into the Las Vegas daylight, when Teffinger hurled his body over the front end.

He slammed into the windshield, flew over the top of the cab, and landed in the bed.

Jackie skidded to a stop and shouted through the broken rear window, "Get out!"

"No!"

She punched the clutch.

Teffinger slid back hard into the tailgate.

The truck accelerated.

Then it was out of the parking garage and the sun was on his face and the heat was beating down and the casinos were sweeping past.

43

Teffinger stayed down, partly to keep from getting swung out but mostly to avoid drawing attention to someone in the back of a truck, a surefire way to get pulled over.

The casinos fell behind.

The buzz got less thick.

Telephone poles rose up.

Then even the fringes of the city disappeared and the Nevada desert took over.

Jackie didn't pull over.

She let Teffinger suffer.

She let the sun have him.

She let the devil's breath suck the moisture out of his body.

That was fine with him.

He'd rather be here than anywhere else in the universe; because here, Jackie would have to pull over sooner or later. Teffinger would have one last chance to make his case with her.

Then it happened.

A raggedy roadside rest area appeared up ahead.

Jackie swung into it, squealed to a stop under the one and only tree, and killed the engine.

No other vehicles were around.

Teffinger climbed out.

His body was a wreck, more than he realized.

Jackie ignored him and headed for the woman's side of small brick building, slowing only enough to cast an evil look before swinging a door open and disappearing inside.

Teffinger eased onto a splintery picnic table and waited.

When the woman came out, Teffinger said, "We have something. I don't think we should throw it away. I think we should work through it."

Jackie frowned.

"Nice words," she said. "Now say the words you really want to."

Teffinger screwed confusion onto his face.

"I don't understand—"

"Yes you do. It's simple. Say the words that are really on your mind."

He hesitated, then he said, "Fine. Did you kill that lawyer back in Chicago?"

"And by *that lawyer* you're talking about Grayson Everly."

Teffinger nodded.

Jackie sat down next to him, exhaled and said, "I'll tell you a few things on one condition—you don't tell another living soul, not anyone, for one week. After that, I don't care."

Teffinger shook his head.

"I can't promise that."

"Then you're not going to hear what I have to say."

The woman got up and headed for Thumper.

"Wait," Teffinger said. "Okay."

"Okay?"

"Yeah, okay."

"Say it."

"I promise."

"Promise what?"

"I promise I won't tell anyone what you're going to tell me for at least one week."

"That includes that Chicago detective, Vic Vine," Jackie said.

Teffinger nodded.

"I won't give you up. I promise. So tell me, did you kill him?"

Jackie put her hand on his knee and said, "I wish we'd met in simpler times."

44

T here was a guy by the name of John Winterfield," Jackie said. "He grew up in Chicago. One of his buddies was someone named Grayson Everly."

"The dead lawyer."

The woman nodded.

"As often happens with friends, they ended up going their separate ways. Grayson Everly went to college and became a lawyer and lived a pretty straight life. Winterfield, on the other hand, took a road slightly less traveled. Do you remember when we went from 1999 to 2000, and it was a big exciting midnight on December 31, 1999?"

"Yeah, right."

"Well, on that midnight, like a lot of places, there was a big celebration taking place in Oxford, England, with lots of fireworks and the like. During those festivities, someone broke into the Ashmolean Museum; they came in through the roof. They left with a painting by Cezanne called View of Auvers-sur-Oise. Unlike a lot of French impressionism pieces which are actually pretty crappy, this one was a nice piece visually, a landscape, and was considered important because it was painted in that transition period between Cezanne's early years and his mature style. It eventually became one of the top ten art crimes. I always suspected that John Winterfield was behind the theft."

"The lawyer's friend."

She nodded.

"The painting didn't go on the market. I would have heard about it. Someone had stashed it and was waiting for things to cool, or a better price, or whatever. I tried to locate Winterfield, to see if he was the one who stole it and if so whether I could broker it for him, but I couldn't find him. It was like he had dropped off the face of the earth."

"Okay."

"Then, finally, I got a lead. It turned out that he'd gotten himself in trouble screwing the wrong little boys in Bangkok," she said. "He ended up in a Thai prison. I went there to see him. He was in bad shape physically and still had a lot of hard time in front of him. It was pretty clear he was going to die in there if he didn't get out fast. He confessed to me that he was in fact the one who stole the Cezanne. He'd stashed it with his old friend in Chicago, Grayson Everly. He asked me to get it and sell it. I'd get 15 percent and distribute the other 85 percent in equal parts to Winterfield and the lawyer. That would be enough for Winterfield to buy his way out of prison and would give the lawyer a nice reward for stashing the painting all those years."

"Sounds reasonable."

"It was," Jackie said. "I got the painting from the lawyer and sold it for roughly eight million dollars. The money went into one of my accounts in the Caymans. Before I could make the distribution, Winterfield died in prison."

"Ouch."

"Fuck him," Jackie said. "He deserved it. In any event,

though, there was his share to deal with. I met with Grayson Everly regarding how to proceed. My position was that we split it. His position was that all of Winterfield's share should go to him."

"Quite the dilemma."

Jackie nodded.

"Negotiations went on, and the longer they did, the more intense everything got," she said. "The lawyer did a lot of checking on me. He found out that I was wanted in several countries. He threatened to take me down. It all ended in a meeting one night in his house. He struck me and swore to the devil that he'd make sure I ended up rotting in jail, and that was it."

"You killed him—" Teffinger said.

She nodded.

"Yeah, I killed him. It happened before I even knew what I was doing. I slit his throat. Then, I carved on his chest, to make it look like some kind of maniac did it. I wiped the place clean and left."

Teffinger pictured it.

He could see the blood squiring from the man's neck.

He could see Jackie ripping the man's shirt open.

He could see her carving the knife in the man's chest.

45

Teffinger stood up.

The sun hit his face and bounced the images from his brain.

He could overlook the fact that Jackie was a black marketer. He could overlook the fact that she was wanted. He could overlook the fact that her past would catch up with her sooner or later and, when it did, things would get ugly, both in her life and his. He could overlook the fact that she bashed the trucker's head in with a rock; if anything, that was almost a mercy killing; and, in fact, it was what the guy wanted.

The lawyer, though—

The lawyer.

That was different.

That, stripped to its ugly raw essence, was nothing more than murder for money. Plus, she might be putting a spin on it; in the end, she ended up with all eight million. Maybe that was her plan all along. Hell, who knows? Maybe she even paid someone to kill Winterfield in prison and had plans all along to kill the lawyer too.

Whatever the truth was, it was way over the line.

It was murder for money, at the least.

He let his eyes fall on her.

She looked different now.

"You're right," he said.

"About what?"

"That we should have met in simpler times." He exhaled and added, "Don't worry about that promise. I'll be keeping it."

She nodded.

"Thanks."

"I don't know if I'll ever tell anyone."

She hugged him.

"I want you to," she said. "Tell the detective, Vine. I don't want it eating at you."

He shrugged.

Then he said, "I guess this is where we say our good-byes."

She kissed him on the lips, ran a finger down his chest and said, "You'll be okay?"

He nodded.

"Eventually."

"Okay, then. I'm sorry I am who I am. I know you wanted more. It was never there to give you. Forget about me."

She got in Thumper.

Through the window she said, "Take care of yourself, Nick."

Then she was gone.

46

Teffinger sat in the dirt with his back against the tree, empty as the devil's soul, but at least free from the uncertainty of what would happen after he and Jackie reached L.A. That was it, for love. He wasn't going to go after it again. It was too uncertain, too out of his control, too messed up. He wasn't built for it. He never would be.

Time passed.

Not a single vehicle pulled into the rest stop.

He didn't care.

He wasn't eager to get back to Denver.

Maybe he'd just hitchhike to L.A. and get on a plane to Tokyo or Tahiti or Shanghai, or anyplace else that was the opposite of his current life, someplace he could think and get his balance and maybe meet someone who had a few kind words for him.

Suddenly something strange happened.

A vehicle passed by on the highway heading south, a red vehicle, a red Camry to be exact.

He recognized the driver.

It was London Stone.

He was positive of it.

Was this some kind of fate?

Was the universe aligning the two of them?

He reached for his phone to give her a call, picturing her swinging back to get him, and then the two of them driving off to who-knows-where with the air conditioning blasting and a Beach Boys song on the radio, maybe Don't Worry Baby.

His phone wasn't in his pocket.

He quickly checked his others, then the ground and all around.

The stupid thing was nowhere.

It must have worked its way out during all the bouncing and shifting and bobbling in the back of Thumper. Fate, huh? What a laugh. He picked up the biggest rock he could hold and hurled it at the restroom with all his might. It ricocheted off the bricks, split in two and fell unceremoniously to the dirt.

He walked over to the drinking fountain to see if it worked. It did.

It wasn't cold but it was water.

He took a long, long swallow, then dumped handfuls on his head until his hair was as wet as if it had been two miles underwater. His shirt was drenched. It was the first good feeling he'd had since Jackie pulled away.

Still, damn, it should have worked out.

What was he with women, cursed?

He sat back down in the dirt.

The picnic table would have been more comfortable but he didn't ever want to get on it again.

Minutes passed.

Then something unexpected happened.

A black BMW passed by on the highway heading south.

The windows were tinted; so was the rear license plate.

He couldn't see who was inside but the vehicle was identical to the one that followed London out of the parking garage earlier this morning.

His heart raced.

It was those two guys; he could feel it.

They were making their play.

They were going for her.

They were finally away from all the cameras and prying eyes of Vegas.

They were free to do what they were going to do.

He got to his feet and trotted for the road.

London!

Hold on, baby!

He made it to the road and stuck his thumb out.

Traffic was minimal.

The cars that did exist didn't stop.

Faces flew past, staring at him in defense mode as they did.

He knew what they saw.

They saw a man all alone out in the desert; a man with a raw bruised face; a man with scraggly dripping hair and a soaked shirt, presumably from stinky sweat; a man in filthy clothes and a desperate look on his face.

Shit, he wouldn't stop either.

Another car came.

This time Teffinger waved his arms frantically.

The faces inside showed horror.

The vehicle actually swerved into the opposing lane as it

passed.

Minutes went by.

No one stopped or even came close.

Then the deep rumble of a motorcycle grabbed his attention.

He turned to find a lone biker pulling off the highway into the rest stop. At the handlebars was a large muscular man in his prime, mid-thirties or thereabouts, wearing colors with no shirt underneath. His hair was long and black, wrapped in a red bandanna up top. His arms and chest were heavily tattooed. Everything about him screamed fuck you.

He pulled next to the building and killed the engine.

Teffinger made his way over.

The bike was a black Harley-Davidson with a fat rear tire, an older model, not in particularly good shape. 1%er was hand-painted on the gas tank with a rough red brush. The tires were nearly bald. The handgrips were wrapped in black electrical tape.

The key was in the ignition.

Teffinger quietly got on and eased the kickstand up.

Then he pulled the clutch lever in and turned the key.

The engine immediately fired at full roar and the seat shook as if possessed.

He popped the clutch.

Instead of taking off, the bike lunged forward violently for a few feet and then jerked to a stop in a death stall. He fired it up again and took off slower.

"Hey, asshole!"

Teffinger turned to see the biker coming out the door with a face full of hate and a neck full of popping veins, frantically pulling a pistol from under his jeans down by the boots.

Teffinger twisted the throttle and braced for a bullet in his back.

Then the shots came.

Bam!

Bam!

Bam!

47

A bullet flew past Teffinger's head so close that he actually heard it over the rumble of the engine as it shot past. A second bullet hit the bike somewhere in the back. Three missed and then another hit the bike. If any more were fired, Teffinger was too far away to hear them.

Then he was on the highway with an open throttle and out of distance.

The speedometer didn't work but the tach did and he kept it just under redline.

The bike shook with a demonic hand, possibly on the verge of explosion.

He didn't ease up.

London was way ahead of him by now.

He flew past cars.

If they were doing seventy-five he was doing at least a hundred, probably more.

He had no glasses.

His eyes were squinted to slits.

If a bug hit him at this speed, he'd be blinded.

The desert barreled past.

The heat was incredible.

The tires had to be close to rupturing. If the back one went, he might be able to muscle the bike to a stop. The front one, though, that would get him an end-o.

He didn't ease up.

Screw it.

Screw everything.

Miles passed like seconds and then something strange happened. A red car up ahead was parked on the shoulder of the road. It looked like London's car.

Teffinger slowed down only to find that the brakes hardly existed.

His plan was to pull up behind it but he was still going so fast that it took him another fifty yards to stop.

The vehicle was definitely a Camry.

He killed the engine, got the bike braced on the kickstand and ran back.

"London!"

No one was there.

The topography was flat; he could easily see a far ways into it—no one was out there, only brush and rocks.

The doors were locked.

The tires were fine; none of them were flat.

No dents showed but a deep black gouge was dug into the front panel—from the BMW?

Nothing showed inside the interior; no keys, no purse, no luggage; no nothing, except on closer look a pop can and a pair of sunglasses.

He shattered the driver's window with a rock.

Inside, the pop can was a diet Mountain Dew, half full.

That's what London liked.

He drank what was left and checked the sunglasses. They

were expensive designer things, obviously feminine, the exact kind London would wear.

He popped the trunk.

There was nothing in there.

He popped the hood.

Nothing was wet with antifreeze or oil.

Everything looked normal.

Nothing looked broken.

He grabbed the sunglasses and trotted back to the bike to find it lying on its side, the victim of a kickstand that had sunk into the asphalt.

It took three tries to get it up.

Then he was back on the road at full throttle.

Hold on, baby.

Hold on.

48

Mile after mile clicked off with no sign of London or the BMW. An exit for an overpass approached, leading to what appeared to be a barren local crossroad. There were no gas stations or other signs of life at the junction. Teffinger swept by without any more interest when something caught his eye. It looked like an old truck up there, sitting still, maybe parked.

Thumper?

He put his muscle to the brakes, slowing the bike to eighty, sixty and below as he went under the overpass, enough to make a right turn up the backside of the exit.

He headed the wrong way up to the top.

Then his heart pounded.

The truck was in fact Thumper.

He pulled behind it, killed the engine and rocked the bike back a little to where the kickstand would come down on a rock.

No one was there.

On the passenger's side floor were two purses.

One was Jackie's.

Inside it were the envelopes of money as well as the

gun—the Glock they took from the trucker. Jackie's suitcase was in the bed.

He surveyed the distance.

What he saw he could hardly believe.

A hundred yards or so into the desert, two figures were in a standup fight, as if they were each trying to wrestle something from the hands of the other.

He ran that way.

"Hey!"

A gunshot rang out.

Both figures dropped to the ground and continued in a desperate battle.

Teffinger ran even faster, bringing his knees higher and fighting through the pain and the heat. Sweat flooded into his eyes. He didn't slow to wipe it or even to squint it out.

He could see the figures now.

One was Jackie.

The other was London.

Suddenly London made a move that got her on top, straddling Jackie's chest. She found a rock at her side, and raised it with both hands to smash in Jackie's face.

Teffinger dived, knocking her hard and sending her flying.

His head impacted the rock.

Colors exploded.

He didn't have time to pass out.

He couldn't.

He forced himself to stay conscious and tried to get to his feet. His legs wobbled and he fell back to the desert floor.

When he looked up, Jackie had a gun in hand, wildly

swinging it from him to London and back again.

"Don't anyone move!" she screamed.

49

A gunshot rang out, but it wasn't from Jackie's hand. It came from Thumper's direction. Walking towards them at a brisk pace were four bikers. One of them was the biker from the rest stop, the one with the red bandanna. The others were dirty variations. All wore colors with no shirts underneath.

As they came up, one of them leveled a weapon at Jackie's head and said, "Drop the gun, bitch! You got two seconds."

She didn't hesitate.

She opened her fingers and let it fall.

It landed with a dull thud.

"Kick it."

She complied and then stepped back.

The red-bandanna guy had a long knife in his hand.

So did another one.

They got on each side of Teffinger, circling, while the other two stayed back.

One of the other bikers said, "To the death," and tossed a knife to the ground at Teffinger's feet.

He grabbed it.

Before he could even raise it into a defending position, both of them charged.

Teffinger swung a wild fist at the man closest to his front.

It landed with the force of a hammer, straight into the man's face. He fell backwards with the impact and didn't move when he hit the ground.

He looked dead.

Teffinger twisted around, got his knife up and kept the red-bandanna at bay.

"You bitch!"

The two bikers that had been standing back both pulled knives.

The three of them got Teffinger in a circle.

There was no way out.

He twisted wildly, this way and that, never letting up his guard in any one direction for more than a nanosecond. The men didn't give up ground but held back.

They were enjoying the show.

They were snakes about to eat a rat.

Let the rodent squirm.

Then, like lightning, the red bandanna charged. Teffinger hurled his knife at him. It did a lightning rotation and then landed in the man's chest hard, blade first.

Blood squirted, lots and lots of blood.

The man teetered for a second and then dropped to the ground.

Teffinger dived at him, pulled the knife out of his chest, and rolled.

The other two bikers were already rushing at him.

Then a gunshot rang out.

It came from Jackie's hand.

He eyes were wild.

"Don't anyone fucking move!"

DAY SIX

July 12
Monday

50

Mid-afternoon on Monday, Stocks & Blondes in downtown Chicago was mostly deserted. The lunch crowd had already left. The after-work drinkers had yet to arrive. Teffinger sat at the end of the bar peeling the label off a second bottle of Bud Light.

The door opened and a man walked in, somewhat hesitantly, letting his eyes adjust.

He was average everything—average looks, average build, average presence—and a little older than Teffinger pictured, about fifty-five, which was fine because it meant he'd been around the block.

He scouted the room, saw Teffinger looking at him, and headed over.

"Nick Teffinger?"

"Right. That would make you Vic Vine."

The man sat down.

"It would."

"Thanks for taking this meeting away from the office," Teffinger said. "You want a drink?"

"You're kidding, right? I'm Irish."

Teffinger smiled.

Vine got a whiskey, got Teffinger a fresh Bud, and they moved over to a more private table by the windows.

"I wanted to do this in person because I had to get my eyeballs on you first and figure out if I could trust you," Teffinger said. "I think I can."

"You can," Vine said.

"Okay. Everything I'm going to tell you is off the record."

Vine nodded.

"Agreed."

"I'm going to tell you some stuff but I won't be able to tell you much about how I got it all. All I'm trying to do is point you in the right direction."

"Nothing will come back to bite you," Vine said. "You have my word."

"Okay, then," Teffinger said.

He took a long swallow from the bottle.

"On December 31, 1999, the big new years eve going into 2000, a Cezanne painting called View of Auvers-sur-Oise was stolen out of a museum in Oxford, England, by a man named John Winterfield. Winterfield, in turn, was a longtime childhood friend of your dead lawyer, Grayson Everly. To make a long story short, the lawyer ended up with possession of the painting, holding it in trust for his friend, Winterfield, who subsequently managed to get himself locked up in a Thai prison."

"I never heard of any of this."

"No reason you should have," Teffinger said. "Anyway, enter a woman named London Stone, who can best be described as a professional mistress. She targets rich married men, digs around to see what she can get out of them, then leaves after she gets it. She targeted Grayson Everly, got him into some serious pillow talk, and learned about the Cezanne. Then she talked him into selling it. London said she'd take care of all the details and Grayson wouldn't be involved at all, so there was no risk to his law license. He agreed to that and, in fact, was a little bit relieved to get rid of it. They also came to a business arrangement. The broker—which they would have to get—would get 15 percent of the sales price; London would get 35 percent, for having to get involved in a criminal undertaking; and Grayson would get the other 50 percent, to keep for himself or to split with Winterfield or whatever."

"Did Winterfield know this was going on?"

"No. My guess is that Grayson didn't worry too much about him because the guy was on death's door. Anyway, London ended up getting in touch with a broker who could handle a project this big, a woman—let's just call her Jackie, with no last name."

"Fine."

"So, the sale takes place. Jackie sells it for roughly eight million dollars. The money first goes into her account in-full in the Caymans, and then she transferred the other 85 percent to a separate account set up by London. Jackie was out of it at that point."

"I'm following you," Vine said.

Teffinger took a sip.

It was ice-cold, good stuff.

"Anyway," he said, "a week or so went past and then London calls Jackie and says she got into an argument with the lawyer, who now wanted a bigger percentage than his 50 percent; he wanted 75 percent, arguing that London hardly did anything and he'd been harboring the painting for years.

He got aggressive, attacked her in a rage, and she defended herself, ending up slitting his throat and then carving on his chest to make it look like some maniac did it."

"So Grayson Everly got killed by this woman, London Stone?"

Teffinger nodded.

"Right."

Vine looked confused, as to how Teffinger could possibly know all this.

Teffinger said, "I'm not done yet. Anyway, at that point, London told Jackie that she was worried that the cops would find out that Grayson had a mistress and would then run down that lead in connection with his murder."

"She was worried about getting caught—"

"Exactly," Teffinger said. "She told Jackie she came up with a plan. What she wanted to do was set Jackie up as the killer."

Vine laughed.

"No one would ever agree to do something like that."

Teffinger shook his head.

"You're wrong. London's plan was that Jackie would get set up as the killer. London would then split the 85 percent with her evenly, which meant that each would get about 3.4 million. Jackie agreed, and here's why. First, obviously, the money was huge, but also because she was already on the run for a number of art crimes, so it wasn't like disappearing would be an inconvenience. Lastly, she had one trick up her sleeve—she had an alibi for the time when the murder was committed, so she'd never actually get convicted."

Vine contemplated it.

"Okay."

"So here's what happened next," Teffinger said. "London Stone knows me. We met in a nightclub last year, we became bed-buddies; it was fun but never serious. She knew I was a detective. The plan was for Jackie to make contact with me seemingly by accident, then fed me enough clues to make me think that she was the killer, which I would then relay to the detective in charge—you—being the boy scout that I am."

"London used you."

"They both did," Teffinger said. "Very well, too. Jackie picked me up in a bar one night and we made love. She said she was just passing through town. She planted a purse with money and a gun in it, for me to find. I was so infatuated that I wanted to tag along. She said fine and we took off."

"What if she'd said, no?"

"Well, that didn't happen," Teffinger said. "But I'm sure she would have just come up with an excuse to stay in Denver and feed me the lies there. In any event, we headed west in her truck and she fed me lies on the way, increasingly making me think she killed the lawyer until, one day, she actually confessed to it. That's when I lost interest in her and we parted ways."

"You don't date killers?"

Teffinger smiled.

"Not that often," he said. "It turned out, though, that London had more on her mind than just getting a stand-in for the killing—she wanted a *dead* stand-in. She hired a couple of guys to take Jackie out. They made a try after London thought that I had all the clues I needed to eventually tell you that Jackie was the killer—but it didn't go the way it was planned."

"Why, what happened?"

"That's one of the things I can't get into," Teffinger said. "When that failed, London went to Plan B. Me and Jackie were in Vegas at the time, and London came to town to meet with Jackie and finalize the plan. Jackie would formally confess the murder to me, no doubt knowing I'd part ways with her at that point, which I did. The two women were then going to meet up on the road; London would abandon her car, and the two of them would continue to L.A. in Jackie's truck—named Thumper, by the way—where London had supposedly set up an escape for Jackie. On the drive, though, London pulled off onto an exit and marched Jackie out into the desert to shoot her."

"To keep all the money for herself—"

Teffinger nodded.

"That, plus now have Jackie irrevocably set up as the killer, and never able to pull her alibi out of the pocket and put London back in jeopardy, being dead."

"Clever."

"Yes, but it didn't go as planned," Teffinger said. "Jackie made a grab for the gun and the two women ended up in a fight. London was just about to bash Jackie's head in with a rock when I showed up and knocked her off. Then Jackie got the gun. She made London confess to me that London was actually the one who killed the lawyer. London also confessed that she was the one who just now tried to kill Jackie, and not the opposite. That fit the facts, too, because Jackie's gun—a Glock—was still in her purse, and the gun out there with us was a Comanche revolver."

"So, where is London Stone right now?"

Teffinger shrugged.

"We just left her there in the desert."

"Still alive?"

"Yes."

"Jackie didn't kill her?"

"No," Teffinger said. "I'm assuming she ended up hitching a ride somewhere and disappearing. I'm only telling you all this so that you didn't end up digging into it to the point where you thought Jackie was the killer. She wasn't, it was London."

Vine shook his head in wonder.

"That's quite a story. I don't know how I'll ever piece it together with evidence, especially if I have to keep you out of it."

"I doubt that you ever can," Teffinger said. "But at least you know what happened and won't be spinning your wheels for the next two years." He drained what was left of the bottle, set it carefully on the table, took one last look at Vine and said, "Don't break your promise to me."

"I won't."

"Forget the name Jackie."

"Jackie? What's a Jackie?"

Teffinger smiled.

Then he was gone.

51

Outside, the Chicago streets were windy, muggy and hot. Teffinger walked for two blocks, made sure no one was following him, and headed for an old pick-up truck in a parking lot.

Jackie studied his face as he closed the gap and slipped in the passenger seat.

"Well, how'd it go?"

"Good," he said. "Vine knows the truth about what happened."

She patted his knee, fired up the engine and said, "So now where to?"

He shrugged. "I don't care. Surprise me."

She looked at him hard.

"If you're really serious about that, I have some business waiting for me in Hong Kong."

He considered it.

"Hong Kong; never been there."

"You'd like it," she said. "It's nice."

He leaned back, closed his eyes, thought what it would be like to leave his job, and said, "Let's find out."

"Are you serious?"

"Dead serious."

DAY NINE

July 15
Thursday

52

Between late starts, endless flights, time changes and a world with no shortage of chaos, Teffinger and Jackie didn't get to Hong Kong until Thursday morning, landing just after daybreak. They got a nice room at the InterContinental on the Kowloon side of the harbor, showered, made love and hit the sack. Two hours into sleep, they were woken by a knock at the door.

Jackie answered.

A heavily tattooed Asian man said in English, "You are Jackie Jones?"

"Yes."

He handed her a package and said, "This is for you."

Then he was gone.

Inside the package was a 9mm Smith & Wesson Pro Series handgun with a full clip. There was no note or explanation.

"It has to be from my contact," she said. "I'm starting to think this project may be a little more dangerous than I was led to believe."

Teffinger soured his face with concern.

"We should get rid of it, and I mean right now," he said.

"The weapons laws here are brutal. This is jail time just waiting to happen."

She nodded.

"I agree. What's the best way?"

"I don't know," he said. "Maybe wipe it clean and drop it in the harbor. It's right outside the door—minimum distance, minimum time, minimum risk."

"Except tons of people," she said.

That was true.

"We'll wait until after dark," he said.

"Okay. That's as good a plan as any."

An hour later the phone rang.

It was Jackie's contact, a man named Kang, who represented the seller.

"At midnight, a driver will come to pick you up. He'll have you put on a blindfold and take you to the painting. You can verify that it's authentic. Afterwards, he'll take you back. The whole thing will take about two hours."

"Okay. Hey, wait, are you still there?"

He wasn't.

The line was already dead.

She looked at Teffinger and said, "I'm free until midnight. You want to go check out the city?"

"I'm dying to."

As a precaution, he wiped the gun clean of fingerprints, then unscrewed the cover of an air vent in the bedroom near the floor, tucked the weapon inside, carefully screwed the cover back in place and then thoroughly wiped his fingerprints off both the cover and the screws. Even if someone found the stupid thing, it could have been put there by any one of the room's prior occupants, going back years.

"There," he said. "You know what?"

"No, what?"

"Something just dawned on me," he said. "There was a guy killed in Denver a little over a year ago, his name was Michael Brown. Someone shot him in the back of the head and then carved something on his chest. It wasn't the same thing that was carved on the Chicago lawyer's chest, but it was a carving nonetheless. At first I wondered if the cases might be related and concluded they weren't. But now I'm starting to wonder—"

"How so?"

"Well, it was shortly after the guy got killed that London and I met in a nightclub," he said. "I wonder if she was the one who killed the guy and then later got into my life on purpose because I was in charge of the case. What do you think?"

"About whether she killed the guy?"

"Yeah."

Jackie shrugged.

"She killed the lawyer in Chicago," she said. "She tried to kill me. Who know how far back she goes?"

"Yeah, it's interesting."

"But even if she did kill the guy, why would she want to get into your life?"

"To monitor things," Teffinger said. "To see if anyone was closing in on her."

"Well, it's a theory. It's definitely something to think about," Jackie said.

"Yeah."

They took in the sights of Hong Kong, had dinner, slept a

few hours and then got dressed shortly after dark. It was time to get rid of the gun.

Teffinger retrieved it from the air vent and Jackie stuck it in her purse. All they had to do was get down to the lobby, walk out the front door and then down to the pier. Then, *splash*, it would drown to death.

They made it to the lobby.

The made it to the harbor, no problem.

Then they walked down a pier.

It was dark out.

No one was around.

They were home free.

The lights of Hong Kong reflected on the waters but the immediate vicinity was dark.

Forty steps from the end, Teffinger said, "There's something I've been wondering about."

"Yeah, what?"

"Well, the 85 percent."

"What do you mean?"

"Well, the reason you agreed to set yourself up as the killer was because London had that 85 percent of the eight million, and she was going to cut you in for half of it. Right?"

"Yeah."

"Three-point-four million. But you never got paid. You never got your half—"

"That's true."

"I've been wondering why."

"Because we all split ways," she said. "You were there."

"Right, I was," Teffinger said. "You had the gun on everyone. You made the bikers leave, and the three of us were the only one's left—you, me and London. You made London tell me the truth about everything."

"Right."

"Then you and me got in Thumper and left."

"Right. That's why I never got paid. We left."

"What I don't understand is, why didn't you right then and there make London get on the phone and make a money transfer to your account?"

"It never even crossed my mind," she said. "You were there, Nick. Everything was frantic and the sun was a demon and my brain wasn't working and neither was yours. We both just wanted to get the fuck out of there and that's what we did. That was all there was to it."

Teffinger nodded.

"That's true," he said. "But then, you never mentioned it afterwards, about how you got screwed."

The woman stopped walking.

"What are you getting at, Nick?"

He sat down on the pier and stared at the reflections. Then he looked up at her and said, "What I'm getting at is that you're the one who killed the lawyer, not London."

"What? Are you crazy?"

"I wish I was," Teffinger said. "You never made London give you half the money, and never complained about it afterwards, because you had the money all along. After you sold the painting and got the eight million, you never transferred anything to London or the lawyer or anyone else. Instead, you killed the lawyer."

"Nick, that's insane."

"I wish it was," he said. "London was the man's mistress, I believe that much was true; and how you and her exactly hooked up after you killed the lawyer, I'm still not sure. But the two of you came up with a plan, which was to initially make me think that you were the killer, only to put on a second charade where I would find out that London was really the killer, and then I would tell that story to Vic Vine." He shook his head. "I'll admit; I fell for it."

He turned and looked up at her.

She had the gun out of her purse and in her hand.

Teffinger turned his head back to the water.

"So what happened afterwards? You gave London a cut of the money for setting herself up as the killer?"

Jackie hesitated.

Then she said, "That's right."

"How much?"

"Half of the 85 percent."

"Three-point-four million."

"Right."

She stepped back out of range from any sudden movement Teffinger might make and pointed the weapon at him.

"God, Nick, you're too smart for your own good."

He looked up and into the barrel.

"So now what?" he said.

"Nick, I never wanted it to get to this."

Teffinger nodded.

"Yeah."

She sobbed.

Her face contorted with pain.

"Nick, I can't go to jail."

"I know."

"I really do love you," she said.

"I know. Me too."

Then Jackie pulled the trigger.

Bam!

53

Teffinger's head didn't splatter.

Jackie pulled the trigger again and again and again.

Bam!

Bam!

Bam!

Teffinger said, "It's not going to work. Those are blanks."

"No!"

She fired again, twice.

The gun exploded but Teffinger didn't fall.

"I'm the one who had the gun delivered," he said. "I needed to know what you'd do. Now I know." He got to his feet, turned and walked away, then said over his shoulder, "If I were you, I'd just throw it in the water."

As he walked away he heard a splash.

Then he was gone.

ABOUT THE AUTHOR

Jim Michael Hansen (also writing under the pen name R.J. Jagger) is the author of over 25 hard-edged mystery and suspense thrillers, including the Nick Teffinger thrillers, the Bryson Wilde thrillers, and the Nicole Stone thrillers. In addition to his own books, he also ghostwrites for a well-known, bestselling author. He is a member of the International Thriller Writers and the Mystery Writers of America. His books can be read in any order.